Defoe Abbott Marx Hardy Melville Montaigne Machiavelli Haggard Chesterton Cooper Emerson Joyce Austen Hugo Eliot Grimm Cooper
Stoker Carroll Christie Maupassant Haggard Byron Molière Schiller
Wilde Garnett Einstein Fitzgerald Hawthorne Smith Kafka Hall
Goethe Dostoyevsky Willis
Baum Cotton Kipling Doyle
Henry Nietzsche
Leslie Dumas Flaubert Turgenev Balzac
Stockton Vatsyayana Crane
Burroughs Verne
Curtis Tocqueville Gogol Vinci
Homer Widger Tolstoy Whitman Busch
Darwin Thoreau Twain Scott
Potter Freud Zola Lawrence Plato Harte
Kant Jowett Stevenson Dickens Burton Hesse
Andersen Cervantes
London Descartes Voltaire Cooke
Poe Aristotle Wells
Hale James Hastings
Bunner Shakespeare Irving
Richter Chambers da
Doré Dante Chekhov Shaw Benedict Alcott
Swift Pushkin
Wodehouse Newton

 tredition®

tredition was established in 2006 by Sandra Latusseck and Soenke Schulz. Based in Hamburg, Germany, tredition offers publishing solutions to authors and publishing houses, combined with world-wide distribution of printed and digital book content. tredition is uniquely positioned to enable authors and publishing houses to create books on their own terms and without conventional manufacturing risks.

For more information please visit: www.tredition.com

TREDITION CLASSICS

This book is part of the TREDITION CLASSICS series. The creators of this series are united by passion for literature and driven by the intention of making all public domain books available in printed format again - worldwide. Most TREDITION CLASSICS titles have been out of print and off the bookstore shelves for decades. At tredition we believe that a great book never goes out of style and that its value is eternal. Several mostly non-profit literature projects provide content to tredition. To support their good work, tredition donates a portion of the proceeds from each sold copy. As a reader of a TREDITION CLASSICS book, you support our mission to save many of the amazing works of world literature from oblivion. See all available books at www.tredition.com.

Project Gutenberg

The content for this book has been graciously provided by Project Gutenberg. Project Gutenberg is a non-profit organization founded by Michael Hart in 1971 at the University of Illinois. The mission of Project Gutenberg is simple: To encourage the creation and distribution of eBooks. Project Gutenberg is the first and largest collection of public domain eBooks.

The Smart Set Correspondence & Conversations

Clyde Fitch

Imprint

This book is part of TREDITION CLASSICS

Author: Clyde Fitch
Cover design: Buchgut, Berlin – Germany

Publisher: tredition GmbH, Hamburg - Germany
ISBN: 978-3-8472-1437-3

www.tredition.com
www.tredition.de

THE SMART SET

Correspondence
&
Conversations

By

CLYDE FITCH

1897

CHICAGO & NEW YORK
HERBERT S. STONE & CO

TO

"MUMSY"

TO WHOM I OWE EVERYTHING FROM THE LITTLE
BEGINNING OF MY LIFE
NEW YORK
1897

The Makeway Ball

Five Letters

- From Wm. H. Makeway
- From Mrs. Makeway
- From Miss Makeway
- From a Guest
- From an Uninvited

The Smart Set

I

From Wm. H. Makeway to Joseph K. Makeway, of Denver.

New York, Jan. 12, 189–.

My Dear Brother:

You did well to stay West. Would to God I had! Julia's big party came off last night. I told her weeks ago, when she began insinuating it, that if it must be it must be, of course, and that I would pay all the bills, but I wished it distinctly understood I wouldn't have anything else to do with it. She assured me that nothing whatever would be expected of me. Unfortunately, she wasn't the only woman with an American husband, and that people would understand. She promised me I should have a voice in the matter of cigars and champagne—you can know they were *all right*—and I believe the success of the party was, in a great measure, due to them.

My having "nothing whatever to do" with it consisted in hearing nothing else discussed for days, and on the night in question having no room I could call my own, my bedroom being devoted to the men (of course you know that Julia and I haven't shared the same room for years, not since the six months she spent with her married sister, Lady Glenwill), my own sanctum down stairs was turned into a smoker, and I was obliged to hang around in any place I could find, all ready for the guests a couple of hours before they began to arrive. Of course, too, she finally bulldozed me into helping her receive. You see, the little woman really was worn out, for she had overseen everything. She is a wonder! There isn't an English servant in New York, or London, either, who can teach her anything, altho' our second footman happens to have been with the Duke of Cambridge at one time. Not that I care a damn about such things—except that the Duke is a soldier—but in speaking of them I get to taking Julia's point of view. I helped her receive some of the people, to sort of give her a feeling of not having the whole infernal thing on her own shoulders. Everybody Julia wanted came, and a great many she didn't want. I suppose out where you live you don't have to ask the people you don't want. Here it's much more likely you can't ask the people you do want. I have some business friends,

first-rate fellows, with good looking, dressy wives, but Julia bars
them every one because they aren't fashionables. You ought to see
me when *I'm* fashionable! The most miserable specimen you ever
saw. I look just like one of the figures in a plate in a tailor's window,
labeled "latest autumn fashions," and I feel like one, too.

Julia looked stunning! By Jove! she was the handsomest woman
there. There isn't another in New York anywhere near her age who
can touch her. They say every one asked about her in London when
she went out with her sister in English society, and I don't wonder.
You know she has a tall crown of diamonds—tiaras, they call
them—I've always been ashamed to tell you before! She came home
with it from Tiffany's one day, and said it was my birthday present
to her, and I let it go at that. Well, last night no Duchess could have
worn the same sort of thing any better. The young one, too, looked
as pretty as a — — whatever you like, only it must be damned pretty! It was her first ball, you know; she's a — —, you know what, it's
her first time in society. She had more bouquets than Patti used to
get when you and I were running about town. And she was as un-
concerned about it! She's fashionable enough—I only hope she isn't
too much so. I don't want her to marry this young Lord who's hang-
ing around, and I say so three times a day. The "young'un" says I'd
better wait till he's asked her, but I don't dare. Julia's fixed on it. She
won't even argue with me, so you can imagine how determined she
is. But I want my daughter to marry an American, and live in her
own home where her father and mother live. One thing, I know:
most of these marrying foreigners that come over here want money,
and I'll be hanged if I'll give the young'un a penny if she takes this
one. I mean it. I give you my word. He led the cotillon with her last
night. I wouldn't watch it. I staid in my den and helped smoke the
cigars. None better! I can tell you that!

Well, good bye, old man. If you hear of any thing good out your
way to drop a couple of hundred thousand in, let me know—better
wire me. Politics have played the deuce with my Utahs. Julia sends
her love, and wants me to enclose you yards of newspaper clippings
about the party. Ha! Ha! Not by a damn sight! It's enough that I was
bored to death by it! The "young'un" often speaks of you. She is
getting togged out to go with her mother and do the town in the
way of At Homes and such things. What a life! Yet they seem to

enjoy it, and pity us. Us! In Wall street! The Elysian Fields of America! Can I do anything for you here? You know I am always glad of a chance.

Your affectionate brother,

Will.

How about that girl you were running after? Why don't you give it all up? You know what a bad lot she is. Settle down and marry. It's the only real happiness. Believe your old brother.

II

Letter from Mrs. Wm. H. Makeway to Lady Glenwill, of London.

Thursday.

My Darling Tina:

It is over, and my dear, I'm dead! Only—*such* a success! Surpassed my wildest dreams! If you had *only* been here. In the first place every one of any consequence in New York came; except, of course, those who are in mourning. There are certain people who have always held off from me, you know; but they've come around at last, and were all in evidence last night and in their best clothes, and *all* their jewels, and you know that always speaks well for the hostess. I wore my tiara that Will so generously gave me my last birthday (of course he hates it himself, but I brought it home, and he had to give in—the Dear!). My wedding necklace, three strings of real pearls, and one string of those "Orient" things we bought on Bond St.—no one could ever tell the difference except Will, who makes a fuss every time I wear them. He swears he will give me a new real string if I put them on again, but I tell him we must economize now to make up for what the party cost. My dress was charming. Grace Nott brought it over from Pacquin for her mother, and meanwhile this cruel indecent new tariff came on! Get down on your knees, my dear, and be grateful you don't live in this wretched country which is being turned into one great picnicking ground for the working classes. The custom house wanted to make Grace pay an awful duty, and then, fortunately for me, but of course it was terrible for them, something in Wall Street went up instead of down, or vice versa (I never can understand those things), and the poor Notts went to smash. The dress was to be left in the custom house. When I heard about it I bought it, duties and all. My dear girl, it fitted me like a dream. Did you ever hear anything like it? Of course, Mrs. Nott never could have squeezed herself into it, so it's just as well she didn't try! It is the new color, and made in the very latest way — in fact, the coming spring mode. I really think Will's description is the best. I'll try to quote it to you: "It begins at the top — *i.e.* decidedly below the shoulders — to be one kind of a dress, changes its mind somewhere midway, and ends out another sort altogether. One side starts off in one direction, but comes to grief and a big jewel, somewhere in the back. The other side, taking warning, starts off in an absolutely different way, color, and effect, and explodes at the waist under the opposite arm in a diamond sunburst and a knot of tulle, on accidentally meeting its opponent half." It really is quite like that, too! Will is as amusing as ever. And he was *so* sweet about the party. Of course, at first, I had to be very diplomatic and get his consent without his knowing. He still hates society in the most unreasonable manner; would even rather stay at home quietly than go to his club. But last night he accepted the inevitable and behaved like a prince. I wonder how many couples in New York who have been married nineteen years are as happy as Will and I are? He made a great fuss, of course, about the champagne and cigars. You would have thought the whole fate of the ball depended upon them; and I must say they cost a ridiculous price. However, he pays for them, and they made him happier; so I don't complain. I am sure, after all, he enjoyed the ball thoroughly, too. You could see it in his face. And what perfect manners he has! Do you remember? Will may not be "smart," but he's a gentleman, and his grandfathers before him were gentlemen, and that always tells.

We don't seem to have had many grandfathers, my dear — of our own, I mean, of course. I know you've married a wonderful collection of them, dating back to goodness knows when, but it isn't so important for American women; they can acquire breeding in their own lifetime. I know no other nation whose women can do the same, and even our men haven't the same ability. Look at the American duchesses — don't they grace even the parties at Marlborough

House? Look at yourself, my dear girl. But you won't, because you're too modest. Still you must acknowledge your success in England is conspicuous. Will's manners are perhaps a little old-school, but that's much better than the new-school. Young men's manners nowadays are becoming atrocious, and I'm sorry to say I think they get them from England. The first thing one knows the only gentlemen left in America will be the women. But I hope American men *won't* lose their reputation—deserved, you must acknowledge—of being the most courteous men in the world to women. Well, to go back to the ball. Of course, all my feelings outside my guests were centered in Helen. I might as well tell you at once, she is considered the most attractive debutante of the year—not by me, I don't mean, nor by my friends, but by the people who hate us, and *everybody*. I think she is very like you, a sort of *distingué* air that you always had. I sometimes wonder if some of our grandmothers (for even if we didn't have grandfathers we must have had grandmothers), if some *one* of them—hope not *two*—didn't make a wee slip once when royal personages were about! Of course there is no use boasting of royal blood in one's veins when it has no business there, but that would account for certain things. You may remember the old portrait of mother's mother. She looked a perfect duchess. Helen can have a title if she wants it. I might as well tell you now. Please find out all you can for me about young Lord – –. He will be Duke of – – when his father or some one dies; so find out if you can, too, how long you think it will probably be before he becomes a duke. And is he rich or poor? He needn't be rich, but I don't want to think it's Helen's money he's after. I'm doing all I can to bring about the match, and yet I'm not so worldly after all as to want a daughter of mine to make a loveless marriage. Helen isn't exactly pretty, but she's extremely attractive. Her figure is perfect, and she's the most stylish thing in the world. I am very happy today as I think that I have *lancéed* her in the best New York can offer. It has not been all downhill work. Her father's name entitled her to it; but he hated society, so he was more of a drawback than anything else. I couldn't boast of any social position in Buffalo, and it's extraordinary how well that was known here. However, the fact of my being of a good, sterling, unpretentious family did help in the end, when I got started, and people saw I was serious about "getting in." Of course, you gave us our first big push forward, you darling. An *entrée* into smart

English society doesn't mean so much for a New Yorker nowadays as it used to, but it means a good deal. And a sister-in-law of Lord Glenwill is a desirable person to know when in London, so it is wise to take her up at home, and I, always having Helen's future in mind, took advantage of every possibility. Perhaps I shouldn't have had to push my way so much here if the Prince of Wales were still *making* an American girl each season, but you know for several years now he seems to have given it up. I think he was discouraged by the last two he made at Homburg; neither of them had any success here the following winter, "hall-marked" as they were, and even London hasn't found them husbands yet.

Of course, as to one of them, I remember the gossip you wrote me about Colonel − −. But, as you said, he had a wife and other incumbrances; so the least said about that the better.

Under any circumstance, I think it's a much bigger triumph to give Helen all New York first, now, simply by our own right, and then this May we'll take her to an early drawing-room, and see what happens next. I shall depend upon you, dear, to see that we go to one of the Princess' drawing-rooms, and don't get palmed off on one of the Princess Christian's or anything of that sort.

Helen was dressed very simply, of course, and no jewels, but looked so sweet. Lord − − was devotion itself all evening. Naturally every one is on the *qui vive* for the engagement, but that's all right. They danced the cotillon together. We had charming favors, not too extravagant—that's such wretched taste—but things we bought in Venice last year, and Hungarian things, and some Russian, and a set of tiny gold things Tiffany got up especially for us.

I had several people down from Buffalo, and mother, of course. I wish you could have seen her, bless her heart. She had on all her old lace, and my coiffeur did her hair beautifully. She looked so handsome, and Will insisted on her dancing a figure of a quadrille with him, and how graceful and dignified she was. You would have been very proud. I was. Lots of people asked about her, and some seemed so surprised when they heard she was my mother. How rude people are; and what did they expect my mother to be like? After all, do *I* look like the daughter of a washerwoman? I think not. We might ask the Grand Duke − −, if we meet him again at Aix.

You know I told Will about my small, timid flirtation with the Russian, and really he seemed proud of my absurd little conquest! A convenient husband for some women we know, wouldn't he be? Ah, but then you see *they* wouldn't deserve him!

Sherry did my supper. He imported some birds from Austria especially for it, and invented some dishes of his own. I think it was all right. People said so, but, of course, you can't believe people. I can vouch at any rate for the serving of it. It was like magic. We seated *every one* at little tables which seemed to come up thro' the floors. They were everywhere except in the ball-room; that was left clear.

We've built the ball-room since you were over. Will bought the house next to us (such a sum as they asked when they heard *we* wanted it!) and the whole lower floor we made into a ball-room. It just holds my series of Gobelins we bought for that outrageous price two years ago in Paris at the Marquis de Shotteau's sale. For flowers, I had quantities of gorgeous palms and lovely cut flowers in bowls and vases wherever it was possible. That was all, — I hate this stuffing a house with half-fading flowers, it always suggests a funeral to me, with the banked-up mantels for coffins. It's horrid, I know, but I can't help it. However, if I am writing in this vein it's time I stopped. My letter is abnormally long as it is — I hope the right number of stamps will be put on it. Forgive me for mentioning it, my dear, but we always have to pay double postage due on your epistles. I don't mind at all — they are quite worth it — only I thought you might like to know.

I have all the newspapers about the ball for you, but I will wait till after Thursday and then send them on in a package. I want to see what *Town Topics* will say. Nobody cares, of course, only you don't like to see horrid things about you in print. Sometimes it treats me very well, and it's devoted to Helen, but once in a while it's atrocious. I'm only a little worried about Lord — —. I don't want it to say I am after him for Helen, because I am *not*! If the English papers have anything in, please send them over — I know some articles are going to be written. If there are any of them absurd and extravagant accounts, of course you will take pains to contradict them. The English press seems often determined to make American society ridiculous.

Will says we will be greatly indebted to your husband if he will get us a house for the season, as you proposed. Carleton House Terrace, if possible; if not, use your own judgment, only not Grosvenor Square—they make too much fun of strangers who go there. I hope you are well and taking some sort of care of yourself, which you know you never do. And please, if you go to Paris at Easter, be sure to write us at once if sleeves are still growing smaller, if hats are big or little, and whether it's feathers or flowers, or both. Also, of course, anything else that will help us. And don't forget to find out all you can about Lord — —. And do you advise announcing the engagement before her presentation, or afterward? And by no means say a word to anybody, as he hasn't proposed yet. By the way, Will is violently opposed to it. But I think Helen and I together will be too much for him, and if absolutely necessary *my health* can give out! That had to happen, you remember, before I could get him out of 15th street and up here.

My love to the Hon. Bertha. How is the dear child? I long to see you. Say what you like, this society life isn't altogether satisfactory. I think after Helen is happily married—to whomever it is—I shall drift quietly out of it, and gradually take to playing Joan to Will's Darby. I'm sure Will would *love* it.

Love to you both, and a heart full to yourself, Tina, dearest.

Your affectionate old sister,

Mary.

P.S.—Don't laugh at what I said about a society life. Of course I don't mean it. I don't believe I could live without it now. I'm tired after the ball, that's all. To tell the truth I don't quite know where my head is. I shall take two phœnacetine powders right away. Do you know about them; they're so good. Did I ask you if you went to Paris Easter to be sure and write me if sleeves— — O yes, I remember, I did.

III

From Miss Makeway to Miss Blanche Matheson in Rome.

Thursday.

My darling Blanche:

Of course I know you are having a wonderful time in Rome with Royalties and all sorts of smart people and gay entertainments, but still I wish you had been at our ball last night. I believe you would have enjoyed it. I don't think anyone can deny we know how to give balls in America, and mama is a wonder! You know she's been fishing for guests for this ball for years. And she wouldn't give it till she was sure of a list of people who would be present that would bear comparison with anybody's; and, my dear, we had it! And I am sure mama feels more than repaid. With such a culmination everything has been worth while—the French *chef* and his terrible extravagances, for you must pay to be known as a good house to dine at—all the deadly afternoon parties, all the exorbitant fees paid for years to the opera singers to sing, the house at Newport—and the one at Lennox, the seasons in London, that shooting box in Scotland (it bored us to death), it was all worth while now that we have arrived at the toppest top. And no one could become her position better than mama. A society matron of the first water is certainly her *métier*.

Lord − − is very much struck with mama. I will tell you about him later. Of course poor papa looks a little what that amusing young Englishman would call perhaps 1872. He wasn't in it for a minute; bored to death, poor thing. You know he hates parties. Thank heaven I am "out" at last, for now I can go to everything that comes on. And do as I please, that is if I want to, because I may marry soon! I wish I could see your expression when you read that. Of course it is Lord − −. He proposed last night, but I told him he must wait, and propose again in a couple of weeks. I wasn't ready to decide yet. I must be free "out" for a couple of weeks at least.

He will be Duke of − −, some day. As the Duchess I shall have precedence over Mamie Smith, Gertrude Strong, and Irene van Worth, and even over all the older women who have married abroad, except the Duchesses of − − and − −. Think what fun it would be to sail in everywhere ahead of Mamie Smith, after all the insufferable airs she has put on! I don't believe I could make a better match. Besides he's youngish and good-looking, has splendid estates, and I really like him. I mean I think he is the sort of man you can get very romantic about. And of course there's no real social life anywhere but abroad, and there's no other life that wouldn't bore me to death. It's only natural, for my whole childhood was spent in an atmosphere of searching after it. Ever since I can remember the chief occupation and interest of mama was how diplomatically to get into the smartest set with dignity. It seemed as difficult as the proverbial camel and eye of a needle and the rich man getting into heaven, and in my younger days the three were all very much mixed up together in my mind. I think I should prefer London to Paris. Smart life in Paris seems to be so very much more immoral than in London, judging from what one hears and the books one reads, and you know I don't care about immorality. I get that from mama, too. She is shocked all the time in the "world," over here even, tho' she tries to hide it.

Our house looked lovely last night. We had powdered footmen, and just enough music and just enough supper and just enough people. One of the secrets of success in society is not to overcrowd anything.

Of course there were some drawbacks to the ball, but small things that didn't really count. Mary Farnham came and sat the whole evening thro', as usual, without once dancing. Even papa said he "drew the line at that." Why doesn't she take something? You see lots of things advertised that change people almost as big as she into a perfect shadow in no time. You feel so sorry for her when she's your guest. I had a great mind to put Lord — — to the test, but I didn't quite dare! Then Tommy Baggs came and repeated his customary gymnastics—waltzed on everybody's toes in the rooms (slipper sellers ought to pay him a commission), tore two women's gowns nearly off their waists and spilled champagne frappé down Mrs. Carton's back; would have ruined her bodice, if she'd had any on, at the back. She bore it like a lamb. Her teeth were fairly chattering, but she laughed and said it was rather pleasant.

Good heavens! Who do you suppose is down stairs? Lord — —! It's going to be a bore if he's coming every day. I shall go down and tell him these two weeks I am to have a complete holiday.

Do write me all you're doing.

With love always,

Helen.

Later — I have accepted him! He was so perfectly charming! I couldn't help it!

IV

From a Guest.

Thursday.

My dear Claire:

I was so glad to hear from you about Florida, and, as you are having such an amusing time, and as the season here is practically finished now that the much-talked of Makeway ball is over, I've decided to join you next week. Besides, I've missed you awfully, and it will be so nice to be with you again. Will you be so good as to engage my rooms for me? — a bedroom with two windows facing south; not near the elevator by any means; not above the third floor — *but not on the first.* Please see that the coloring is blue or pink; I'm not particular about design or material, or anything of that sort (I don't think people should be too *exigeant*) — only yellow, or red, or white, or green rooms are too awfully unbecoming to me. Have drawing-room to connect with the bedroom please, and then a room for my maid. I hope you won't have to pay more than seven dollars a week for her (all included, naturally). She isn't at all particular. I'm sure I couldn't afford to keep her if she were, and she's such a treasure. Of course she reads all my letters and minds my own business more than I do myself, and uses up my crested writing paper at a terrific rate; but that one expects — don't you think so — with a *good* servant?

I know you are mad to hear all about the ball, so I'll tell you. In the first place it was a great success, and that settles it! The Makeways are now a power in New York society, and there's really no reason why they shouldn't be. His family are all right and her English connections are better; and then what a charming woman she is! She makes a perfect hostess. Such tact! Everything was carried out in the best of taste. If they erred at all it was on the side of simplicity; and yet that gives you a wrong idea about the ball, because it really could boast of splendor. Yes, I mean it, but of a solid, real kind. There is nothing papier maché about the Makeway house; nor about its owners, nor about their entertainment. You can't help but believe this, and it gives you a sense of social security! Everyone anyone would want in their house was there. If any line was drawn tightly inside the smart circle, it defined the pseudo-déclassé. Mrs. Makeway might be described in England as a slightly early-Victorian hostess, or if our presidents had at all the position and social power of royalties, she would be ticketed perhaps as of the Hayes period, except that would imply "Total Abstinence," which would mean instant death to anyone in smart society, thank goodness! I suppose you've heard that old *mot* of the dinners at the White House during the Hayes administration, that water flowed like champagne! Well, that will never be said of the Makeways. Their wine was the very best, too; I never had better at any party, seldom as good, and even John, who scoffs at the idea of women being a judge of wines, confesses, that, though we've entertained everybody all our lives, we've never had such a good wine inside our doors. The supper was, in the first place, comfortable, and, in the second place, faultless. (There was a queer kind of game, which I loathed, but of course I knew, whatever it was, under the circumstances it was the right thing, so I choked it down.) The music was superb—all the good Hungarian orchestras in town. The cotillon favors were lovely, and some very stunning gold and jeweled things from Tiffany's must have cost a fortune.

But of course what you want to know about most is the people and what they had on. I wore my—but you'll see my dress in Florida, so never mind. Mrs. Makeway had a superb dress, but she always dresses handsomely. What a nice man Mr. Makeway is. You felt sure he was bored to death by the party, and all of us at it, but he concealed it with such charming manners and such natural courtesy that you really felt somehow it was a pleasure to come and put him out. The daughter is a great success; there's no denying that. She has a perfect figure, and is very graceful. She seems to have her father's manners, brought up to date by her mother. She's going to be a leader, you can tell that, and apparently she can be an eventual duchess, if she wishes. Young Lord — — is still here, and his devotion in the Makeway quarter is undisguised. Everyone likes him, and says he isn't the sort of young fellow to be merely after her money; but no one can tell if Helen is going to take him or not. I am sure of one thing, she will do as she pleases.

There were beautiful jewels in evidence at the ball. Mrs. Makeway wore, I believe, a dozen strings of the most gorgeous pearls. All *real*, of course, with their money. They must represent a fortune in themselves. Poor old Mrs. Hammond Blake came with *all* her Switzerland amethysts, and a few new topazes mixed in (she must have been at Lucerne last summer). She looked like one of those glass gas-lit signs. But really, all the best jewels in New York were there. And it is wonderful to see how the women whose throats are going the way of the world have welcomed the revival of black velvet if they haven't the pearl collarettes. I shall be wanting something of the sort myself soon. Woe is me! And John does keep looking so abominally young. I tell him out of courtesy to me he must get old more quickly, or people will be saying I married a man years younger than myself!

John says I needn't trouble to furnish people with subjects for talking; they can make up their own. But I don't think we are gossips nowadays here in America; do you? Which reminds me that everybody says the Mathews are going to separate at last. She's going to Dakota, and get it on incaptability, or cruelty, or some little thing like that. Everybody wondered at first why, since she'd stood it so long, she was going to divorce Ned now, at this late day, but it has leaked out. Think of it—Charlie Harris! Aren't you surprised? It's only about two years since *he* divorced his wife. Mrs. Harris got the children, so I presume Mrs. Mathews will keep hers to give Charlie in place of his own. If I remember the number he will be getting compound interest! You know the Mathews babies came with such lightning rapidity we lost count. One was always confusing the last baby with the one that came before it. Anyway, I think Charlie Harris gets the best of it; so, even if it isn't altogether ideal to possess your children "ready made," as it were, still Elsie Mathews is a charming woman, and I never could bear Mrs. Harris. She told such awful fibs, and her exaggerations were not decorative; they were criminal. Why, I couldn't recognize a piece of news I told her myself when I heard her repeating it to some one else not five minutes after, as John says.

Heavens! for the third time, "as John says," I must stop. But *I am* a very happy married woman! John gives me everything I want, and I adore him.

When I hear from you I will telegraph my train. We missed you awfully at the Makeways. John spoke of it several times. He loves to dance with you because you are always ready to sit it out and do all the talking. Dear me, I'm afraid that doesn't sound complimentary, but I assure you he *meant* it as such!

How nice it will be to be with you. You aren't strict about your mourning, are you? I don't think it's at all necessary, way off there.

With love, always affectionately,

Maybel Parke Rodney.

V

From an Uninvited.

Thursday.

My Darling George:

I hope this letter will reach you before you leave Minneapolis. I do wish you would leave politics alone, if they're going to take you away like this. Believe me, the country can get along much better without you than *I* can! When we are married you have *got* to give them up. When we are married, too, and this bore of a divorce of mine is finally settled, I presume I shall be invited to Mrs. Makeway's parties! I wasn't asked last night to her big ball!—not that I care. I am sure that beast of a husband of mine will never be able to prove his nasty charges against us, and that I shall win the case. Then there'll be no excuse for Mrs. Makeway and her prudish set, and I promise you they shall eat "humble pie," if there's any left in the world after all my dear friends have made me devour. Tom has been making overtures to my maid through a detective, but Lena is faithful to us, and I've promised her double any sum they offer her. *When* my position is all right again, I shall go in for society in the most extravagant, splendid way for one long, brilliant, spiteful season, and I shall punish every one of these women who have snubbed me so terribly. After all, half of them owe their positions in the world to my family, and with my family to back me there will be no trouble about my being absolutely reinstated. My people will back me up, too, for we have never had a scandal up till now. We have been almost the only family left.

Of course the papers are full of the Makeway ball, and the pictures of Mrs. Makeway are too deliciously absurd for anything. One looks like that one of me in the Evening News when I gave my evidence. I really believe it's the same picture. I hear that she looked rather well with her famous pearls on (which, between you and me, I believe are false), and her tiara, which all the out-of-town people go to the opera to see. But they say she was dressed entirely too young, and showed she thought her own party a great success. However, what can you expect? She was nobody; her family are most ordinary people, the kind that are prominent in some unfashionable church and influential in its Sunday-school. O, la-la-la-la! She prides herself on having an ancestor of some sort who fought in the War of Independence—a common soldier, I suppose, in Washington's army; that's why she has had an office in the "Daughters of the Revolution." *We* had several ancestors in the war—commissioned officers; and they all fought for King George, thank heaven; and if they had only won my father would have been the third Lord Banner, probably, if not something better. So hang Mrs. Makeway! Her daughter is an ugly little creature; she hasn't a single feature that doesn't go its own way irrespective of the others, and with a total disregard for the *tout ensemble* of the poor girl's face. You know the sort of thing—each feature seems to be minding the other's business. Her teeth *look* lovely, but I believe some of them are "crowns"—they do that sort of thing so well nowadays! What I will grant her is a beautiful figure, but my corset-maker, who is hers, too, gives me her word of honor she laces awfully! They say she had the best time of any girl at the ball; which, if you ask me, I think beastly taste.

The house everyone says looked very beautiful—of course, money will do everything—and the music was superb for the same reason, and the supper not too extravagant. (I suppose they economized on that!) But lots of people I've met say they were bored to death, and that there was an awful crowd. It's extraordinary the people she had there! How she got them I don't know—all the swells. But dear me, after all, that's nothing; swells will go to any-one who'll amuse them. I hear old Makeway looked fearfully miser-able, and, instead of paying other women compliments, made love to his own wife all the evening. It's extraordinary, because he is really a gentleman. His great-grandfather and my great-grandfather were great chums; made their money, I think, in the same business.

By the way, the Pinkertons have written me that they have still more evidence against Tom. They say *she* is "doing a turn"—whatever that is—in some variety theatre. According to accounts she *did* Tom for a good deal—just served him right.

Do hurry back—I miss you so, and am so lonely. It's a year and a half since we've been separated so long as this. Come back. Don't make me jealous or *suspicious*. Besides it isn't complimentary to *trust* me so tremendously.

The lawyer is here—I hope he has come to assure me of my posi-tive victory.

He has thrown up the suit. We are lost! He says Tom has indis-putable proof, and that there is no use trying. Can Lina be a wretch after all? or do you suppose it is your man? Come at once, at no matter what sacrifice. The Majestic sails on Wednesday. Hadn't we better throw up the sponge and take it?

Always, and in spite of everything, your adoring

Edith.

The Plaintiff

Two Letters

From Mr. John Stuart Kennington to Mrs. Kennington, his wife.

From Mrs. John Stuart Kennington, by special messenger, to the law firm of Jordan & Fields.

I

From John Stuart Kennington to Mrs. Kennington, his wife.

Newport, October —th, 189-.

Suspicion is absolutely foreign to my nature. Therefore, far from a thought of worry when I found my business visits to New York this summer becoming more and more easy to make as far as you were concerned, I used instead to get "a lump in my throat" on the train which left you here behind, believing that your love for me influenced you to hide your own feelings and aid me all you could in the performance of my duties, even at the cost of your own preferred pleasure and at the price of a good many hours of loneliness. Loneliness! Oh, what fools we men sometimes are! Yes, and how careless you women become!

I shall never forget the day I changed my plans suddenly, deciding I wouldn't go to New York that week after all, although my bag was packed and Smithers already at the station with it. The instantaneous look of disappointment which leaped across your face, and which for some seconds you didn't sufficiently realize to conceal— what a vista that look opened out to me—a hellish vista! And your constrained little smile—a sort of conscious visible movement of the muscles about your mouth—"on purpose"—came too late. That first look had been like a Röntgen ray over the last six months of our life—lives I should say, for while you and I were living one life, you at the same time, without me, were living another. Then I understood this summer's comfortable weekly good-byes, so different from other years! I think, down in the bottom of my heart, I understood *all* at *that moment,*—though I wouldn't acknowledge it not even in secret to myself, and even when, before another twenty-four hours had passed, my eyes were damnable witnesses against you. I couldn't believe them, and doubt if I would have if you had not confessed. Of course, I knew whenever we had guests Jack Tolby was always one of them, and also one of the guests wherever we went, but it only seemed natural. He was extremely agreeable in our house; it's only now I realize he has always rather avoided me at the club. I suppose even men like him have some sort of conscience, or at least a sense of decency, if not of honor, toward their own friends, and, if so, good God, how ashamed he must have been every time he had to take my hand! And *you*, when you received my lips on yours, already satiated with kisses in my absence! Ugh! Kate! Kate! how I hate you! Yes, hate is the word. And to think *you* are the mother of my children! That is the *big* hurt.

I want you to understand that what I am going to do is entirely for their sake, not at all for yours. You who have been the first to drag the name of Kennington in the public mud. Three honest gen- erations of us have kept it clean and honorable, and our wives have done the same for us all down to you—all except my wife. I used to think that in marrying me you had placed me deeper in your debt than I could ever repay. Ever since the first time I saw you I loved you; and after that meeting I put my arms about no woman—arms that had been free enough before—until I put them around you. And since then the same. I have been an absolutely faithful husband to you. Do you understand what that means? I don't believe so. I preferred you to every other woman in the world. When away from you, your memory guarded my embraces. Yet I am not a romantic man. Now, for instance, I look at it all in a straightforward light. I realize that you were a girl with no money and no particular posi- tion in the world; and in marrying me you obtained both. You have reveled in society—thanks to me and my family—and this is the return you have made. You have dishonored us. Now listen; this is what I propose doing. I do not intend to have my children suffer publicly, as they would, especially my two little daughters, if your disgrace were made public. It happens to be with us that a father's falling in this direction does not so seriously, if at all, affect his chil- dren; therefore, for their sake, instead of my divorcing *you*, I am going to give you proof and witness by which you may divorce *me*, for your own sin. But there are certain conditions with which you must comply. I will send by my lawyer a paper, which you will sign in the presence of witnesses before any further steps are taken. In this paper you will agree on your securing your divorce to marry Tolby. I have had an interview with him (this is not an age nor a country of duels), and I demanded that he make me the reparation of marrying you when you are free. I must frankly say from his manner I do not judge him over anxious. I believe even a duel with pistols would on the whole have pleased Tolby better. It is true that precedent is not in his favor. His own experience with you will doubtless make him a little uneasy. To continue: You are to marry him. You are to demand of me in your suit the sum of $— — (and do not be uneasy, you will win your suit). This will be convenient for you when you re-marry, for you know Tolby hasn't a cent. It will be a real love match on your part, charming! You are to give all my mother's jewels to our oldest daughter on her marriage, and all the jewels I have ever given you to our second on hers. Should the girls not marry at twenty-five, they are then to have the jewels. As to the children I shall have to submit, in my rôle of the guilty party, to letting you have control over them; but I warn you that this is to be only nominal. If ever I find you prejudicing either one of them *against me in any way whatever*—even if I find their affections are being alienated from me by some sort of public opinion or gossip—I warn you that when each one is old enough to understand he shall be told the *truth*. You had better look to it then that my children love me. Your own hold over their affections rests upon it. These points, and a few others bearing upon them, will be set forth legally in the paper which my lawyer will bring you. Kindly send me word if you are prepared to sign, and, if so, when Mr. Jordan or his representative may call. Good bye.

John Stuart Kennington.

II

From Mrs. John Stuart Kennington, by Special Messenger, to the law firm of Jordan & Fields.

No. — East 66th street.

Benj. K. Jordan, Esq.

Dear Sir:

On second thoughts, after you have left me, I have decided to ask you to write Mr. Kennington as follows—I mean I will give you the idea of what I wish said: Acknowledge the receipt of his letter, and say I shall be delighted to sign the paper he proposes at his earliest convenience. I must ask, however, that he submits the document through you, etc. (the same as we agreed on just now in our interview). Now, besides, you must demand for me the following changes or corrections, or whatever is right to call them, in the paper. First, the sum of $— — is too small; $— — must be added to it. Also, I am not willing to give up all my homes. Either the house in New York, or in Newport, or on Long Island must be made over to me. And I positively refuse to part with the ruby necklace to one of my daughters unless I should choose to do so of my own free will. For the other jewels I have no use whatever. You can express that as you see fit. Ask him to let me hear as soon as possible.

Yours truly,

Gertrude Corte Kennington.

Tuesday.

The Summer

A Letter

Grand Hôtel de l'Europe,

Aix-les-Bains,

Sunday.

My Dear Mary:

Our summer has been a perfect failure. I said in the very beginning if we followed John and the children's ideas it would be; but as I was in the minority I gave in. Fortunately we did catch the tail end of the London season. The others wanted to go straight on to Paris, but for that once I put my foot down—and all the trunks as well. It was very warm; still there was a great deal going on, so we didn't mind the heat, at least I didn't. Heat in London during the season is such a different thing from heat in Switzerland or some dull seaside place, where there is not sufficient distraction to take your mind off it. I was doing something every minute. That's the charm of London. Every hour of the day there is something, and if there ever was a dull interval I dropped into one of the picture galleries. You know you have to do that sort of thing over here. People talk about pictures, and some do it very well, too, and you really meet painters out. The children go and see things that are good for their education, you know—the Tower, where Mary Queen of Scots, or Anne Boleyn, I forget which, was beheaded, and the—well, all sorts of places like that. The heat made them rather irritable, and Evelyn had a rash, but I thought it was good for them to see all the historical sights. So we staid on just the same till after Goodwood. And the races ended my pleasure, for next we started for Lucerne.

I said all along there would be no one in the place. Of course people do go there, but on their way to somewhere else, or coming home at odd times, and not for too long. There is never really any society there. I knew it. I have had experience with it. Besides, we know the places that every one does go to in July and August. I preferred Homburg, with Aix at the end, but I would have put up with Trouville first, or Ostend, or even Dinard. But no, Switzerland it was! I hate it; I always did. It's too like its photographs. It has absolutely no style. It's all nature, nature, *nature*! The mountains and lakes, no matter how old they really may be, still always have the *beauté du diable*; and for a woman of my age—who has to resort to art to keep herself looking the slightest little bit younger than she is!—it gets on one's nerves, all this natural beauty! I prefer some *place* that has to resort to art, too, and make itself up a little with gorgeous hotels, casinos, theatres, and baccarat tables. Mountains bore me, and I hate to go on the water. There at Lucerne the mountains stood continually and solemnly around, just like elderly relatives at a family reunion, and the flat lake lies as uninteresting as the conversation of these estimable creatures would be. And then the people! The town crowded to suffocation, scarcely breathing space, and yet *nobody* there. To be sure once in a while one notices an extraordinary old frump go by, who turns out to be the Duchess of this, or Princess that, but I assure you one would have been ashamed to drive in the park with her (at home), unless she was placarded. Now and then somebody decent from New York or Boston arrived on a morning train, but, of course, they usually left in the evening, driven away by the glare, or the white dust, or by the eternal tourists. That man Cook has done more to spoil attractive places than any other dozen people in the world put together. Sometimes, of course, they are amusing. One day I went to see the Lion! Don't laugh. John bet me five hundred dollars I wouldn't go. So, of course, I did. Fortunately I'd heard the children explaining it or I shouldn't have enjoyed so much the following joke.

A woman and her daughter, both Cooks, (tourists I mean, of course, tho' heaven knows what the mother mightn't have been at home), stood in front of the monument.

"What's this, Clara?" asked the older woman.

CLARA.

Why this is the famous Lion of Lucerne, mother!

MOTHER.

Oh is it, ain't it lovely! What's it for—I mean why is it?

CLARA.

Why, you know, mother, for defending poor Marie Antoinette in the Tuilleries!

MOTHER.

Oh, did it! And then people say lions are such nasty, heartless creatures.

CLARA.

(Laughing.) O mother! the lion didn't do it; it's only put up for a monument to the soldiers who died trying to protect her from the mob!

MOTHER.

Oh, I see; it's just a fancy picture! Well, anyway, I think it's awful sad.

What do you think of that? And those are the kind of people Switzerland was full of. Some were alone, and some were impersonally conducted in a very loose sort of way. Wherever you wanted to go they were sure to be ahead, and kicking up a middle-class dust that choked you. The loud sound of their incessant *talk* echoed from snow peak to snow peak. And their terrible clothes, chosen evidently "not to show the dirt" (but they did), came between your eyes and any beauty of scenery there might be, even if you cared to see it, and I didn't. And then the droves of rich Americans at the hotels! Where did they come from? Where did they learn how not to dress? Where did they learn how not to behave? Those are the questions I asked myself continually, and always gave them up! I became so tired of hearing of Pilatus and the Rigi, I felt as if one were at the head of my grave and the other at the foot! I had a sort of indigestion of mountains and lakes! And there was John! rushing out every other minute to sit and look at them (I assure you I was threatened very much with the neuralgia from the damp of the lake terrace). And he climbed everything that was climbable, even preferred walking up; but when there were railways I made him take them for fear he'd hurt himself. I believe he went to the top of every blessed thing that had any top! I found plenty of horrid people to look down on without going to the tops of mountains. I tried to drive, but there wasn't a decent turnout in the place. I went out in a little steam launch, but was frightened to death for fear I'd be run down by one of the steamers crowded with Cooks. Oh, no! *assez* of Switzerland for me! I said to John—"Bring me here to bury me if you like, but don't bring me here alive again." And finally, when he and the children couldn't find anything more to climb, I managed to move them on to Aix, and here I am.

And, of course, the English season has just finished, and the French people haven't begun to come yet, and Aix is hot, and dull, and empty! Really, isn't it trying? There are even only second-rate cocottes about, none of the smart ones yet! I am dying of the blues. Besides I have to take the baths, although I don't want them, because the only way I managed to persuade John to come here was by pretending I *needed* them! When I think of you in Newport, in spite of the heat, leading an absolutely ideal life with your visits, your dinners, and your balls, I am green with envy. These are the times when life seems really almost too complicated to worry through. Or course if I were like John's sister Margaret, sort of half-crazy, who loves the real country, prefers a farmhouse to a hotel, fields and woods to a casino, I might get on well enough. But I consider that nothing short of a morbid state of mind.

If you love me, write me soon, and cheer me up. But don't tell me of too much going on with you, or it will be more than I can bear. If you could honestly say that it was rather a dull season in Newport this year, you don't know what a comfort it would be. I do hope John and the children appreciate the sacrifice I am making for them. I'm sure I try to have them realize it. It only shows what we mothers will do for our children.

With love, your affectionate, but depressed,

Geraldine.

P.S.—Of course, as you can imagine, the shops at Lucerne were filthy. I didn't buy a thing except some presents for the servants. At Aix the shops are better, but with so few people here, somehow one has no inspiration. I've bought literally nothing except five hats.

The Children

Three Dialogues

- Divorce.
- Birth.
- Death.

I

Divorce.

Tom Barnes, *age ten, whose mother, Mrs. Barnes, having divorced his father, her second husband, has since remarried, and is now Mrs. Fenley.*

Claire Worthing, *age seven, whose mother, Mrs. Worthing, having divorced her Father to marry the divorced Mr. Barnes, is now Mrs. Barnes.*

Scene, *a Fashionable Dancing School in New York. A quadrille has been announced. Master Barnes goes up to Miss Claire and bowing somewhat stiffly, mumbles some not altogether intelligible wards. Miss Claire, sliding down from her chair, says "Thank you," with perfect composure and a conventional smile, as, taking his arm, they choose a position in the dance.*

TOM.

Shall we stop here in this set?

CLAIRE.

No! Becky Twines' dress would ruin mine. And she made her maid give her that one on purpose I'm sure, because she knew what I was going to wear. But I don't care. I heard mama say, yesterday, her mother, in spite of all her money, hadn't been able to buy her way into several houses. I don't think she ought to have been invited to join our dancing class at all. When people buy their way into other people's houses like that, how do they do it do you suppose? Does the butler sell tickets at the door, do you think?

TOM.

Perhaps so! Butlers look like that. My! I'd jolly like to be a butler! (*They have moved on to another set.*) Shall we stop here?

CLAIRE.

Oh, no, not here! Teddy Jones always mixes us up. He treads on our toes.

TOM.

Yes, and squeezes the girls' hands, too.

CLAIRE.

Oh, that we don't mind! Would you like to sit this dance out on the stairs? (*She would prefer it herself.*)

TOM.

No, let's dance. Come on, this is a good place.

CLAIRE.

As you please. Do you like kissing games?

TOM.

(*Red in the face.*) No; do you? (*He does.*)

CLAIRE.

Oh, I don't mind. (*An embarrassed pause.*)

TOM.

I like football and those kind of games.

CLAIRE.

They are all very well for boys. But I don't much care for games myself, and, besides, I don't have the time.

TOM.

What do girls do with themselves all the time?

CLAIRE.

Oh! I have my lessons, and I walk out with my maid every morning, and I dress three times a day, and then I have visits to make on other little girls.

TOM.

You've got a new father, haven't you?

CLAIRE.

Yes, mama was married two weeks ago.

TOM.

How do you like him?

CLAIRE.

Oh, very much!

TOM.

You take my word for it, he's a brick. I know! He used to be my father once.

[*The music starts up, and the couples bow.*

II

Birth

Elsie, *age 6.*

Teresa, *age 8.*

Bob, *age 7.*

(*They are sitting on the steps of the large piazza of a beautiful country house, the two little girls affectionately close, the boy at an awkward distance. There has been a pause in the conversation, which the boy breaks.*)

BOB.

We've got a new baby at our house!

(*Splendid effect!*)

ELSIE, TERESA.

(*Together.*) Oh!

(*Their eyes are suddenly bright and their faces glow with a sort of awed curiosity and pleasure, not unmixed with envy.*)

ELSIE.

What kind?

TERESA.

(*Eagerly.*) Yes; which is it?

BOB.

(*Proudly.*) A boy, of course!

(*The two little girls' faces fall for a second, and they are silent, but not for long.*)

ELSIE.

Of course there have to be boys sometimes.

TERESA.

Yes, to make a change.

ELSIE.

Isn't it funny where babies come from!

BOB.

Yes, you find them in cabbages.

ELSIE.

Oh, no! They come down in rainstorms.

TERESA.

No, no! They come out of the flowers.

BOB.

Stuff!

ELSIE.

They do come from the skies, because you know the stars are little babies waiting to be picked.

TERESA.

I thought the stars were the places where God put his fingers through.

BOB.

They aren't any such thing; they're the gold tacks that fasten on the carpet of heaven.

ELSIE.

When I grow up I shall have eleven babies, because I have eleven favorite names, and I shall have them all at once, so they can have nice, happy times playing together, and there won't have to be any horrid older brother and sister, always getting the best of everything.

TERESA.

And I'll tell you what! I'll have eleven children too, to marry yours.

BOB.

No, I'll marry one of them.

ELSIE.

No, you must marry one of us.

BOB.

Which one?

ELSIE.

Well, I think it would be best for you to marry me and be father for my eleven children. I want them to have a father. I love my father.

TERESA.

Yes; but then who'll be a father to my children?

ELSIE.

Yours can be sort of orphans; they needn't ever have had any father.

TERESA.

(*Approaching a tearful state.*) No, that's awfully sad. I want my children to have a father, too!

BOB.

Never mind. I'll be their father besides.

ELSIE.

Let's play house.

TERESA.

Let's!

BOB.

Let's play Indians, and I'll scalp you two girls!

ELSIE.

No, that's too rough. We'll play husband and wife. Bob and I will get married, and, Teresa, you must be the minister and a bridesmaid.

(*They retire into the house, where, with the aid of a wrapper, a night dress, a bouquet, and a black mackintosh, the ceremony is properly performed.*)

ELSIE.

Now we'll have a little girl baby, and (*to Teresa*) you must be it.

TERESA.

No, I want to be the wife now, and you be the baby.

ELSIE.

No, I'll be the husband, and let Bob be the baby.

BOB.

I won't be the baby!

TERESA.

Anyway, it isn't polite for a little baby to come right away like that. They never do.

ELSIE.

That's so; you have to wait till the news that they want one gets up to the skies.

III

Death

Teddy and Elsie are in the drawing-room, which is shadowy and sad with the drawn curtains. The children speak in half whispers, and with an air of importance.

TEDDY.

It's going to be in here.

ELSIE.

Isn't it awful. (*Sobs.*)

TEDDY.

Papa was a brick!

ELSIE.

(*Sob.*) Now he's an angel.

TEDDY.

(*Thoughtfully.*) Do you really think papa would like being an angel?

ELSIE.

Everybody likes to be an angel.

TEDDY.

I don't.

ELSIE.

O Teddy!

TEDDY.

It sounds stupid to me, like Sunday all the week. Besides, papa won't have any office there, and what'll he do without an office?

ELSIE.

Isn't it awful. (*Sob.*) Poor papa!

TEDDY.

(*Swallowing a lump.*) Don't cry!

[*There is a slight noise overhead.*

ELSIE.

O Teddy! What was that?

TEDDY.

(*Trembling.*) Don't be afraid!

(*He puts his arm comfortingly around her, and they sit in a huge arm-chair together.*)

ELSIE.

What is it like to be dead.

TEDDY.

It's like school all the time, never letting out, and no recess.

ELSIE.

(*With another sob.*) Poor papa! Are you afraid of him now?

TEDDY.

No— —

ELSIE.

Do you want to go up and see him?

TEDDY.

No. That isn't him anyway upstairs!

ELSIE.

Yes, it's him; only his soul isn't there.

TEDDY.

Do you believe it? Say, if that's true, how did his soul get out?

ELSIE.

I've thought of that. This is what I believe: When people die, God kisses them, and their soul comes right out of their lips to God's.

TEDDY.

I'll never play be dead with you, anymore.

ELSIE.

No, I don't want to, either.

TEDDY.

God might think I really was dead, and I might lose my soul.

ELSIE.

You can't make believe with God.

TEDDY.

That's so; I forgot. I say, Elsie, I'm never going to be wicked again in all my life.

ELSIE.

Nor I.

TEDDY.

Oh! girls never are wicked. I believe when we die Death comes along and pulls us by our feet; that's why our souls go out. They're afraid of Death.

(*Elsie shudders, and nestles closer to her brother.*)

TEDDY.

Don't be afraid; I won't let him catch you.

ELSIE.

Poor mama, she cries all the time.

TEDDY.

And she won't eat.

ELSIE.

I know where there are some little cakes.

TEDDY.

(*Eagerly.*) Could you get them?

ELSIE.

Not alone. I'm afraid.

TEDDY.

I'll go with you. (*They get down out of the big chair.*) Do we go to school the next day after it?

ELSIE.

Yes; and wear all black. (*Sobs.*) Poor papa.

TEDDY.

(*Choking.*) Don't cry.

ELSIE.

You're crying too.

TEDDY.

No, I ain't! (*Crying.*)

(*She kisses him. He is comforted, but very much ashamed.*)

ELSIE.

Do you think we can go to the circus next week just the same?

TEDDY.

I don't care about circuses now.

ELSIE.

Neither do I. I don't want to go anyway. Let's find the cakes.

TEDDY.

And then we'll make a coach out of the chairs, and you'll drive me four in hand.

[*They go out of the room smiling.*

Maternity
Three Letters and a Cable from Mrs. Stanton,
a Widow

I

To Robert N. Stanton, Esq., her son (and only child)

Venice, Thursday.

My Darling Boy:

Your letter reached me a few moments ago. We were just starting
off to see the Tintorettos in the Scuola, but I opened your envelope
before I stepped into the gondola, and read enough in the first few
lines to let the others go on without me.

First, let me say this; no one in all the world wishes you more joy,
more real happiness, than your mother. I wish it more than anything else in the world, and have prayed for it for you every night of
my life since you first came into this world. And I've always count-
ed a wife for you as one of the chief joys of your future. I have always wanted you to marry, only I have always said to myself — not
yet; I can't spare him yet. Mothers begin their children's lives by
being the most unselfish beings in the world; and then, as we grow
older, I'm afraid we are inclined to go to the other extreme. I won't
tell a falsehood and say I am glad you are going to be married now.
Forgive me, dear, forgive me; but in my heart there is still the same
cry — "Not yet! not yet!"

Oh, I know I'm wrong! It *is* to be, and I accept it; but it seems so
sudden; and, after all, I was so unprepared, and you are my life,
dear — my everything. You must let me sigh just a little; I'll promise
to be all smiles at the wedding. When you first laughed in the sun,
and twinkled your baby eyes at the stars I was not a very happy
woman. You were only six months old when I divorced your father.
(How much I have regretted that step since. It would have been far
better had I borne with him. He was the only man in the world for
me; and he would have come back to me if I had only waited. Then,
instead of dying wretchedly miserable as he did, he might have
been alive to-day, and we would be companions for each other; but
I was proud and wilful — however, enough of that.) As I said: when
you were a tiny baby I was an unhappy woman, with an heart emp-

ty and bruised. How I hugged you to it! O never, *never* can I tell you, nor can you imagine, the comfort, the blessing you became to me! Your butterfly-like little kisses made well all the bruises; your little hands, with their soft, flower-like caresses, smoothed away the troubles, and before long you seemed to have crept in, little body, little soul, into my heart, till you filled it completely. And now I must share—Oh, we *are* selfish, we mothers! for I want all—all! I used to be a little jealous, in those early days, even of your nurse. Do you know, Rob, that I bathed my baby every morning of your little life, so long as you took infant tubs? I wouldn't leave it to any-one else; and for more than one year of your life, in the middle of each night and early morning, I warmed over a little spirit lamp (I have it yet) your preparation of milk, and fed it to you, so that you would get your food from me in one way, if the doctor wouldn't let me feed you as I hungered to do. How soon it was you knew me. I could make you smile when no one else could; and what a joy it was to see a love for me coming into your infantile existence. I had cried a good deal before you were born, and some afterward, first out of relief and then for pure gladness. But under your dear influ-ence I gradually forgot how tears came. You almost never cried; and what a good baby you were—oh, a blessed baby!—and I tried to repay you by not worrying you with too many kisses, with too much loving, which I'm sure is not good for a child. Sometimes I had to clench my hands, so strong was my desire to take you up and clasp you tight. Then how quickly you began to grow; and be-fore long my letters and intimate conversation began to be filled with what "Rob said this morning;" and you did say such delightful things! I never knew so naïvely witty a child! And soon you reached the age when I could play the rôle of comforter. The knocks and bruises I've healed by kissing them!—do you remember one-third? I'm sure I don't. The many imagined slights of your little friends, which were forgotten on my lap! The little aches and pains that were slept away in my arms! How full my life was then! What a blessed boy you were! And then those half-lonely years, when eve-ryone frightened me—by saying you would be spoiled—into send-ing you away to school. I begrudge those months I spent without you yet. But how we enjoyed the vacations! That's when we began reading together again real stories, not those of the younger days. Do you remember your favorite when a very small boy? We always read it when you weren't feeling very well, or after you'd been punished for being naughty, sitting together in the great big old rocking-chair. It was about two poor little fatherless boys whose mother died in a garret, and they were so terribly poor they had to beg a coffin for her, and they alone followed it to the grave. There was a very trying and sad woodcut of the two little orphans doing this, and we always cried together over it. It wasn't a healthy story for a small boy, and I don't know how we got hold of it. Oh yes, I do! It was published by the Tract Society, and had a moral. It was your aunt sent it to you, but I have forgotten the moral. The football period began in the school vacations, and went all through college; but still I think you were always more fond of books and music than athletics; and I was never good at outdoor sports; I only managed to master tennis so as to be able to play with you.

The four years of college had some loneliness in them, too; but I enjoyed my visits to Williamstown, and then is when I began going into "society" a good deal again, for I said when Rob comes out he will want to go. He will have at least three cotillon years, and I want him to go in the best society we have. Besides, there is sure to be a wife; let her be a girl of our own position and class. But the dearest parts of your college life were our four trips abroad during the summer. And then it was that I began to turn the tables, and when *I* was tired to lean on *you*, and when disagreeable things happened to let you take mother in your arms and hold her there till she promised to forget them. Then it was when your judgment began to mature, and I found it so clear and good, and have been guided by it ever since. Oh, those perfect years between the day you graduated and now! How proud I was of you, too, in society. It seemed to me no one was so brilliant a talker at a dinner table. It was all I could ever do to listen to my neighbor instead of straining my ears across the table in your direction. And I am sure it was not maternal prejudice that picked you out in a ball room, for it was not I who made you leader of all the cotillons so long as you cared to dance them. Then how more proud I was of you when you interested yourself in politics. I love my country. Your father fought, and bravely, in the civil war; so did my brother. And I know if such a terrible calamity as another war should befall us, you would be ready. The patriot fights for his country, in peace, in politics, and I am happy to say your interest in our government is as keen and active to-day as ever. Then there is the ever increasing success in your profession— haven't I been through it all with you! Never, I am sure, were a mother and son more sympathetic. The reason I came abroad this year was because I was afraid we were getting too dependent on each other. I realized you now preferred staying home with me evening after evening instead of going out. I loved it, but I knew it was wrong. I argued if I went away for a little you would go out into society again, and to your clubs, seeking companionship. It was not good for a young man—I said to myself—not more than thirty-three, to be spending all of his spare time with an old woman—for practically I am that, though you must never call me so; it would break my heart! And so, though it was really an awful break for me to do it, I went away, and the only thing I wanted to happen did, only more. Oh, yes! more than I wanted—because I didn't want you to marry—not yet! And if I hadn't gone away you would probably never have met this Miss Stone, and you would have been just as happy. For you *were* happy with me before you met her; weren't you? Oh, of course, I know not *so* happy, and not in the same way, but later on you would have met perhaps Miss Stone, or somebody else you would have cared for in the same way; don't you think so? I am afraid, if I let myself, I'd be sorry I went away. And yet no—*no;* I'm not so selfish as all that. If you really have found the one woman in the world for you I will try to be glad. I will be glad. I am glad! There! I am. After all it is your happiness. How unhappy I should feel if you loved her and she hadn't returned your love! Yes, it is much better as it is—for *you,* so it must be for me, too. Allowing even for all a lover's enthusiasm, Miss Stone must be very charming and very lovable. I can see it in her picture, too, which I thank you for sending. Of course, without it I should have been cruelly anxious to see what she was like. She is very pretty—very. I am obliged to confess that. I think I shall come to love her for her own sake, and not only for yours. If only she will love me! You love me more than I deserve or merit, so don't say too much about me or she will be sure to be disappointed.

If I must be a mother-in-law (horrid name), I want to be a nice one and be loved. I shall do my best. Only it is the giving you up. O Rob, darling! What shall I do without you—without my blessed son? Breakfast alone, luncheon alone, dinner alone, everything alone! Ah, I can't bear the thought of it! No! No! I don't mean that! But of course I can't and won't live with you — it's very kind and like you, dear, to say I must, but I don't believe in that. You'll see enough of me, I'm sure, as it is. And I shall have my memories. Baby and boy, you are mine alone. I didn't have to share you then; and I won't have to share the memories now, and no one can take them away from me. And what if you make me a grandmother? It isn't at all sure. Everybody doesn't have babies now, like they used to. Still, if you do! Well, I shall probably adore it. But then I must settle down, wear caps, and perhaps revive a widow's veil. I certainly shall have to be more dignified and not go gallivanting about everywhere, and control some of my enthusiasms, or I shall be a ridiculous old creature. You see, I have always kept your age. Now I must take one awful flying leap to my own; and then go along with myself properly. I shall have to become much more regular about church and know all the saints' days. A good thing that will be for me, too, I'm sure — What do you think? They've just knocked on the door and told me it is dinner time. I've been three hours over this disgraceful letter. I knew I'd been dreaming[1] a good deal between sentences; but I didn't know it was so bad as all that. Well, I'm going down to tell the others my *good* news (you understand that *good*, don't you?), and we'll drink to the health and happiness of you both in some crimson Chianti. And they shall all see how happy I am over your happiness. For I am. And you will see it, too, when I come back; which will be as soon as I can.

Good bye, my boy. Forgive your old mother if she's seemed a little cross in this letter, because she isn't really. I shall write Miss Stone a little letter to-night. God bless you and her (and me), and fill your lives as full of happiness as your hearts can hold and mine can hold for you! Good night, my comfort, you best son in the world!

Your devoted

Mother.

Yes, yes, I *am* glad, dear; so glad. Don't misunderstand my letter. Your mother is glad, honestly and with — yes, I *can* say it now — with *all* her heart.

¹ The words "and crying" are well scratched over, so he couldn't possibly read them.

II

A Cable to her son. (Sent fifteen minutes after the preceding letter.)

Overjoyed, congratulations, love.

Mother.

III

Letter to Miss Lucy Stone, Troy, N.Y.

Venice, Thursday.

My dear Miss Stone:

So you are going to take my boy away from me? I begrudge him, just a little, or just a good deal; but I will tell you a secret. I feel pretty sure that when I know you, I shall be grateful to him, instead of grudging, for giving me you for a daughter; and you must love me, for after all if it wasn't for me you wouldn't have him, would you? He has been a perfect son, and they make perfect husbands. And he loves you, my dear. Oh, if you had any doubts of it—which of course you haven't, or I shouldn't like you—but if you had, could you have read over my shoulder his letter to me to-day telling me about it.

I am very impatient to know you, but I think we shall be great friends, through Rob, before we even meet. Till then believe me your—dear me, what?—your Robert's affectionate old mother.

Katherine Miles Stanton.

I am sending with this a little old jewel I found at an old shop the other day; it is a love ring of the sixteenth century. Perhaps you will find a place for it. I send it with my love.

K. M. S.

IV

Venice, Thursday.

Dear Gertrude:

You will be very much surprised to hear from me, I imagine, as a correspondence is something we could never keep up. But our friendship has lasted without it a long time, my dear girl—forty-two years—for we met when I was fourteen. I haven't forgotten yet how the whole school became bearable after you took possession of the other little white cot in my room. It's a year and a half now since I've seen you, and I've missed you. Troy is so near; and yet, after all, it is so far, too, when we realize how seldom we meet. You must give me a whole winter soon! Yes, for I am going to be alone; Rob is going to marry, and that's why I am writing you. It is to a Miss Lucy Stone, of Troy. Do write me about her. Do you know the family? Are they friends of yours? Rob is fearfully and wonderfully in love; and I can't blame him after seeing her picture. She is lovely (and charmingly dressed), and I am sure Rob would never fall in love with any one but a lady. Still, I want to know if she, or rather her family, are really smart people, or what. Even if they are "what," I'm sure it won't make any difference to Rob, and so it mustn't make any difference to me. But it will be a *relief* to know that they are friends of yours, or even that you know them. I pretend not to believe in class distinctions, and I don't; but when it comes to your own son, somehow or other you do want him to choose his wife among his own social equals. Between you and me I am just about broken-hearted. I know it is very wrong of me, but I had sort of let myself grow very dependent upon him, and always had looked upon his marriage much as one looks upon death, as inevitable, but always remote and the end of all things. It still seems like the end of all things, but in time I shall get used to it. I feel simply ashamed of myself for feeling as I do now. Of course, if it were given me the choice, "your son's happiness, woman, or your own selfish comfort," I wouldn't hesitate a moment, but it's so hard for a mother who has spent such happy years with her son to realize that his happiness does altogether and absolutely depend on some one else, and on that one and no other? And then we always have that terrible doubt,—has he chosen the right woman for him? Just as if he wasn't, after all, the best judge for himself. Of course he is; and in time I know I shall be able to thank God he made this choice, but just now—just to-night—it seems to me I come nearer to envying you your childless wifehood than I would ever have thought possible.

Being in this sentimental, unreal city, doesn't help me any! Forgive this, I'm afraid morbid, letter, and believe me affectionately always—write me the truth—your school girl friend,

Kitty.

Have they any position whatever in Troy?

A Letter of Introduction

Four Letters

- From Mrs. Joslyn of New York to Mrs. Lemaire of Washington.
- The same.
- From Mrs. Lemaire to Mrs. Joslyn.
- From Mr. Hamilton-Locks to the Hon. Forbes Redding of England.

I

Letter from Mrs. Joslyn of New York to Mrs. Lemaire of Washington, unsealed and unstamped.

Friday.

My Dear Mrs. Lemaire:

I am very happy to introduce to you Mr. Hamilton-Locks, of London, a friend of mine, who goes to Washington for the first time. I know I am giving you both a pleasure in bringing you together, and any courtesy you may be able to extend to Mr. Hamilton-Locks will be as if shown to me also.

Always sincerely,

Emily Joslyn.

II

A second Letter from Mrs. Joslyn to Mrs. Lemaire, sent with a special delivery stamp.

Friday.

My Dear Mrs. Lemaire:

I gave a letter of introduction to you to a young Englishman this morning. I hasten to write, and beg you, as far as I am concerned, to pay no attention whatever to it. He was sent over to us by Lady Heton, a traveling acquaintance, whom we know really nothing of, and it's been a great bother trying to be civil and everything else to him. I felt obliged to give him the letter, but you will understand by this that you are to ignore it quite as much as you like. He is no friend of ours whatever, merely an acquaintance that has been forced upon us.

We hear you are having such a gay season in Washington. We think of taking a house there for next winter. Can you manage to keep out of the political set if you want to? I don't mind ambassadors, but I should think all the other people would be most ordinary. I suppose you will come on for the Makeway Ball; won't you? If so, do lunch with me the day after; don't forget.

Yours, ever sincerely,

Emily Joslyn.

III

Letter from Mrs. Lemaire to Mrs. Joslyn.

Wednesday.

My dear Mrs. Joslyn:

Where is your young Englishman? I adore young Englishmen, and why doesn't yours come to see me? Did you give him the letter? He has been in Washington a week, is constantly at the P— —'s, and all the diplomatic corps are entertaining him. The women are mad about him, he's so awfully good-looking.

If you want a house in Washington next winter why not rent ours? We are going to Rome in December.

Yours, always cordially,

Gertrude Lemaire.

IV

Letter from Mr. Hamilton-Locks to the Hon. Forbes Redding.

Washington, January, '97.

My dear Old Chap:

This place is a very good sort, rather like a little English Paris; more cosmopolitan than Boston, I mean, tho' no other city here seems quite so lively as New York. The embassy is giving me no end of a good time. I'm sure I'm more than grateful to your uncle. I find society in this place is more like European without trying to be, while in New York they try more, and *aren't*. New York society has an air of its own, and, I must say, it's a damn fine air, too. Of course, like other places, it has some frumps, and what Blanche Heton meant by giving me a letter to a Mrs. Joslyn is more than meets the eye. But we are not burnt twice by the same flame. The *lady* gave me in turn a letter to some one here, and I was so afraid I'd forget and use it by mistake, or leave it at the woman's door one day when I'd been drinking a good many whiskeys and sodas and didn't care what I did, that I tore it into bits and dropped them in an umbrella stand in Mrs. Joslyn's hall five minutes after she gave it to me. There's no use in running any risks. And when a woman over here *is* stupid she's damn stupid. So is she superlatively fetching when she is charming. And, by Jove! but they know how to draw the line — all but Mrs. Joslyn.

People over on this side think every Englishman comes over after a wife, and at first they pretend to be very haughty and independent, and then if they find out he is not after a wife after all, like your humble servant, they are quite angry about it.

I hope you're keeping an eye on my dogs for me. Love to Millicent.

Yours,

Ted.

Wagner, 1897

A Letter from Lady Aires to the Countess of Upham, at Homburg.

Bayreuth, Aug., 1897.

My dear Rose:

Our stay at Bayreuth is nearly over—the last opera to-morrow; and, to be frank, I am extremely glad, although of course it has been perfectly charming. First we heard Parsifal and the Ring; which is four operas, you know. Why they call them a "Ring" I can't see yet; and I don't like to ask, it gives the musical people who really know the chance to be so superior, and they are conceited enough as it is, goodness knows. Anyone would think it was a disgrace not to have been lullabyed to sleep when a baby by a symphony orchestra! I'm sure it isn't my fault if I don't know which is Schumann and which is Schubert; and what's the difference? (Between you and me I don't care. Of course I adore music, but it's like a great many other things—you mustn't ask too many questions!) Well the first day was "Parsifal." It's a *dear*! Beautiful, perfectly beautiful! I wore my white mulle with my green and white hat, and if I *do* say it (and I must, for I'm sure no one else will say it for me), women are such jealous cats about frocks. I didn't see a better turned out woman. Such a tremendous lot of smart people as are here, too. Really you ought to have come. I'm sure you would have enjoyed it. Between the acts it's quite like Sunday in the park. The entre-acts are very long, giving us a chance to shake out our frocks and wake up and amuse ourselves. Some people go up a little hill, or into some pine woods; but that's rather dull, for you don't meet half so many others—most everyone stays in front of the theatre. But I must tell you about "Parsifal." In the first place it is awfully long. And Parsifal himself is entirely too fat! I am sure such a very good young person as Parsifal shouldn't have a stomach! There are a lot of sort of monks in rather fetching pink red cloaks, with pale bluey gray skirts underneath. (Not at all a bad combination, and gave me an idea for a costume for up the river.) Their chief is ill, and almost always in great pain, but it does not prevent his singing the longest of speeches. Parsifal kills a lovely swan—it flies in *so* naturally. Really Wagner was a most wonderful man! Then there is a Gypsy girl; a sort of snake charmer, who has bottles of things all through the play. I couldn't make out quite if she were Parsifal's mother or what. But she is quite mad, and wears only a very uninteresting old brown dress. I must make this criticism of Wagner: You don't see many pretty dresses in his operas. Then everyone goes to a banqueting hall, which is also partly a church. The scenery moves along in a most miraculous way and the hall is really very lovely. There are children in this scene, and they lift the chalice, and it glows—an electric light in it you know, but it's really lovely. And the music is simply heavenly. I assure you I cried like a baby at this part; I couldn't tell you why, unless it's the poor wretched creature (Am— something his name is; I can't find my programme). He's very handsome. I intend to buy his photograph. He has to lift the holy cup, and he feels he is unfit to do it. He is a sinner and wishes he were dead, and somehow or other you feel awfully sympathetic with him. I know the times I've been to church and knelt down so ashamed I couldn't lift my head, thinking of some of the beastly wicked things I've done in my life. And that's just what the second act is. A crowd of women try to seduce Parsifal, but they are all German chorus women, and it really doesn't seem such a great temptation.

But then the girl who was ugly in the other act comes on very beautiful (but hideously dressed, why don't they get Worth or Doucet, I wonder, to help them?) and she sings a great deal and very loud, and kisses Parsifal, and then everything goes suddenly to wrack and ruin. I shall never dare kiss any very good young man again—not after that! In the last act, this same creature, looking more like Act I., washes Parsifal's feet. I should hate to play that part, but it's all very pretty and affecting, and the music—well there are no words to describe it. And the whole rest of the act is too wonderful! Really you have to cry. Of course, it's too long, and you're awfully hungry, but there is a rather smart restaurant now, where everybody goes afterward to get their spirits back; which reminds me that Mrs. Gordon turned up yesterday and appeared at the restaurant at night, affording us a good deal of amusement. First she started to courtesy to the Royalties, who don't want to be noticed. This she perceived in the middle of her courtesy, and cut it short in a quick way, which made her look exactly as if *something* important in her toilet had burst or broken. Then she flew all over from room to room, trying to find a table that suited her, disturbing the whole atmosphere, like meteors are said to do in the skies, and creating the impression, or trying to, that she owned the entire place. She won't be happy here, for it isn't easy for anyone else to own anything where Frau Wagner is installed; which reminds me to stop this gossip and tell you seriously about the other operas.

The first of the Ring is the Valkyrie; you can remember it because of Lord Dunraven's yacht. And they swim around in the water; which is, I suppose, why he called it so. But no; on second thoughts, that isn't it at all. The first opera is Rheingold, and it's the Rhine maidens that go swimming about. How absurd of Dunraven to have made such a mistake. I like the Rheingold awfully. The first act looks just like water, and the music is so pretty. Then, in the second act, there are two splendid big men—one in white, the other in black bear skins—who are rather fetching. The Rheingold is the least sociable of the operas, as there is no entre-act. But it is fortunately a great deal the shortest. I think it is one of my favorites. I seem to know more what Wagner is about in it. I don't believe he knows himself what he is about some of the time in the Valkyrie. This second opera is awfully long. However, it has two good entre-acts, when you can walk around and talk to everybody; and I can assure you we have plenty to say after having been kept quiet for over an hour in the dark theatre. The chairs are so uncomfortable, and if you move somebody hisses. There is not much politeness in Bayreuth. We don't get as good a view of the stage as some people, but we have splendid places; the Countess of − − is in front of us, her sister right beside me, and behind are the − −s, and near by Lady − −. So you see we couldn't possibly have better seats.

For the Valkyrie I wore a new mauve and pale green frock. I don't think you've seen it. The bill was atrocious. I sha'n't pay it; but the costume is a great success. Portions of this second opera are awfully tiresome, first one couple and then another, going on for hours about nothing, but there are some exquisite clouds that move and grow and scatter exactly like nature, only more so, and make up a little for the dull people. I notice one thing: *all* the gods and goddesses have always such troubles. There isn't a single happy creature among them, not even Wotan, who is god of them all, and wears a silly gold curl over one eye. I think it lowers his whole dignity; but they make a great many mistakes like that. Of course, one oughtn't to think of these things, but should simply listen to and enjoy the beautiful music, but my nature is so sensitive I can't help it. There are a lot of Valkyrie, you know, who wear a sort of antique dress-reform costume, not pretty, and ride through the air on deliciously funny-looking horses. And Brunhilde, the leader of them, a rather nice person, behaves quite like a human being in "Siegfried," the next opera, which I will tell you about later. In "Valkyrie" you think she is going to be burnt up, but in "Siegfried" she is saved after all. I suppose there is some sort of Biblical idea about hell. You recognized the Bible very often in "Parsifal." I much prefer Siegfried as a person to Parsifal. He's not such a *very* good boy. There's more an air of athletics, football, rowing, and all that about Siegfried, while Parsifal smacks just a little, I think, of the Young Men's Christian Association. You can *kiss* Siegfried with impunity, too; in fact, it saved Brunhilde's life, and I wouldn't mind running a few risks myself to be saved in the same way! You get perfectly drunk with this music of the last act of Siegfried. Of course, my dear, you know I am now writing about the *third* opera, "Siegfried." You must follow me closely, for it's very easy to get confused about them. "Siegfried" is awfully long, too, and the first act—well, I don't mind telling you I slept a good deal. You see, the theatre gets so stuffy, and then one is digesting one's luncheon, and the stage is so dark, and I maintain that the music soothes you. I wore, of course, another dress, something quiet, as it was rainy, but I saw no one who looked any better. Between the first and second acts I managed to get a bow and a hand-shake from the Prince, to the visible envy of Mrs. Gordon. I wish you could see the dear beast. She flutters around the royalties every minute, like a nervous bird, and as if they were her nest of eggs and a bad little boy was in the neighborhood. I *hate* snobs; don't you? I am lunching, by the way, with Mrs. G. to-morrow. Quite a big, smart party of us, I hear.

That funny dragon comes in "Siegfried," you know, and of course it is much more amusing here than in Covent Garden or New York. But it's the last act that I *love*! Such passionate music! Brunhilde falls madly in love with Siegfried, who is, of course, ever so many years younger than she. But it's just like us women, especially when we are Brunhilde's age. For I suppose she's forty something, as she was grown up and went to sleep before Siegfried was born, and when he kisses her he seems to be quite a man! By the way, Brunhilde was put to sleep for interfering somehow or other in the love affairs of Siegfried's mother and father, who are really sister and brother. If you think of it, the story is extremely indecent, but operatic things never seem to be shocking; music, apparently, covers a multitude of naughtiness, like charity is reported to do. Very likely that's why Mrs. — — is always doing so much for institutions and what not — for her sins, I suppose. I always thought she was a naughty old hypocrite! By the way, there is a comic character in "Siegfried," and in one of the others, I forget which, called Mime — a funny little dwarf, the sort of thing they put in a Christmas pantomime to amuse the children.

Later.

I have just come from the "Götterdämmerung," the last opera, and I am completely exhausted. I am as if I were in a dream, and can only think and feel and write of this beautiful, beautiful music and scenery. I am absolutely absorbed in it. Some people took the train for Nuremberg right after the performance. I am sure I never could have. I really can't believe they *felt* the thing. Our train goes at 1:45. Such a nice hour; one doesn't have to hurry in the morning, and can have one's hair done properly. I have a charming new way of doing the hair. I got it from a Frenchwoman who sat just in front of me in the theatre to-day, and when it was light enough I studied the arrangement till I got it by heart. You want something like that to do during the long duets. Otherwise your attention is apt to wander from the opera, or you get sleepy. To go back to the opera, it began with the same scene that Siegfried finished with, which was rather disappointing, but a real horse came on and behaved as quiet as a lamb, with Brunhilde screaming like mad all about him. I suppose they put cotton in his ears, or something. The scene changed (without letting us go out for a rest, which I thought something of a sell) to the house, where Siegfried falls in love with another woman (Oh, these men!) I forgot to tell you, my mind is so full of the music, that I wore my new Russell & Allen winter frock, and I caught lots of people taking it in. But, dear me, how badly the German women dress! I haven't seen a single *chic* one among them since I've been here, I don't believe I shall come to Bayreuth again. Besides, the music is too wearing. The Rhine maidens come back in this act! It is most wonderful the way they swim about! But, as far as I can gather, they are rather nasty cats. One thing I will say, though: I think Wagner's on the side of the women; for, in spite of Brunhilde's being in love with little more than a boy, she has all your sympathies. So has Siegfried, too; which is odd. I really sobbed when he died, he was so good-looking, and seemed so sad. This whole opera is very depressing. We reach Munich to-morrow night at 7; and I propose going to the Residenz Theatre there, and seeing a light opera just for contrast. But how bad the shops are at Munich. I believe there are some good pictures, but I think one sees so many pictures in Europe; don't you?

I presume you know Brunhilde behaves rather like Dido in the end: nearly everybody, more or less, is murdered off, and there is a sort of Madame Tussaud exhibition in the clouds at the curtain. Of course, I haven't really given you any sort of an idea about it at all. There are no words that will adequately describe it, only I promised to give you a detailed personal account; and I have done so. The reason we are going to Munich is we can't get a sleeper yet, everything is so crowded. Isn't it disgusting. This last opera is rather too noisy at times, and awfully long—longer than the others. But there's a men's ballet in it that is rather nice; not dancing, you know, but singing and posing and walking about, with imitation bare legs, most of them. But I think the best thing about the opera is it leaves you in such an exalted mood. I know I won't be able to think of small or worldly things for weeks, much less write about them. Before I forget it, be sure and write me if it's true that Mrs. — — and Sir George — — are both at Homburg, at the same hotel. I hear they are, and there's no end of talk about it. But then I find there's no end of talk about everything and everybody. It is not that people mean badly, but one has to pass the time somehow. I think I love best of all the Rheingold music. It is like a jeweller's shop window in Bond street; it seems to shine and glitter and sparkle. You see very few jewels here in Bayreuth; of course, there's very little chance to display them. Women wear the usual small string of pearls. That's about all. As most everyone wore one I wear two, with a different pendant each day. I like to be just a little original, and keep my own individuality.

Well, now I must tumble into bed or I shall lose my beauty sleep. I'd hate to have my figure get like these German singers. I wonder why! I'd have myself strapped between boards—I'd do *something*. Good-bye, my dear. Write me all the gossip you can get a hold of. I haven't sent you any in this, but that you couldn't expect. It was impossible that this letter should be anything but Wagner, Wagner, Wagner. I wish you could have been here with me—you'd have seen heaps of your friends. Of course I ought to tell you one thing, because I felt it myself: there's nothing catchy about the music.

Lovingly,

Fanny.

Art

A Letter

A second Letter from Lady Aires to the Countess of Upham.

Munich.

My dear Rose:

It was very thoughtful of you to write me so soon, and Aubrey and I wish very much we could join you, but our money is all spent and we must hurry back to England, where we can economize by making cheap visits among our friends for a couple of months. In December we go to New York to spend the winter with mother. You never go home, do you?

I am so glad you felt you got so complete an idea of Wagner from my letter. I was a little afraid I hadn't done the whole thing justice, but I assure you there were many more people there than I thought of suggesting, and the operas, tho' long, are very delightful.

Here in Munich the chief thing is the picture gallery, as of course at this time of year all fashionable society is away and the theatres and opera either closed or giving second-rate performances. There are more musées than you really care to visit, and are full of masterpieces, many quite as atrocious as masterpieces so often are. The principal one — its name begins with a P — is the one we've been to.

I wish you could see the Rubens, or else it's the Van Dykes — I forget which, but they are beautiful; and when one thinks how long ago they were painted, it's wonderful, isn't it? One thing awfully interesting about a picture gallery is to see the absurd difference in women's dress now and in former times; don't you think so? And sometimes one gets ideas for one's self.

This particular gallery is altogether one of the most satisfactory I've ever been in. It wasn't crowded full of Baedeker people and that sort of thing. In the second room we went in we met Lord and Lady Jenks and the Countess of Towns. That was the room where we saw a portrait the living image of Janet Cowther. We all shrieked with laughter! You know how she has what my vulgar little brother calls an "ingrowing face" — it sinks in instead of coming out, so that the poor creature can't know what it seems like to have a real profile.

It's extraordinary that there should have been two such faces in the world—don't you think so?—even with two or three hundred years between them. The portrait was painted by—dear me! I can't remember, but it was some one we all know. There's one thing I shouldn't mind, and that is knowing the lady's corset maker; I'd like to give his address to Janet, because, my dear, in spite of her face he had made the lady's figure beautiful. I think that's really the nicest part of a picture gallery—seeing comic likenesses to your friends.

Lady Jenks and I sat down on an uncomfortable bench without any back and talked away for nearly an hour. What an amusing creature she is! Has stories to tell about everybody under the sun. By the way, she vowed you and your husband got on awfully, and only lived together as a matter of form! I took up your cudgels, my dear, and told her it wasn't true in any particular; that Ned adored you and was an angel. Of course, he got drunk—that I knew, as all the world did, but you were used to that. It isn't true, is it? He never struck you? I'm sure he didn't! You'd have told a good friend like me; wouldn't you?

Well, just as Lady Jenks and I finished the others came back from going through all the other rooms. We were everyone of us dead tired, looking at pictures is so fatiguing. We decided to go back to the hotel and have tea in the garden. But I think it is a dear gallery, and to-morrow—we don't leave till the next day—if we've any time left after doing the shops, I intend to go back and see the pictures all over again.

Write to Eaton Sqr.; the servants will forward. Poor things, they must have had a dull summer! They say the heat in town has been fearful! But I don't think servants mind; do you? And then they have the run of the house. I am sure they use the drawing-room and sleep in my bed!

Good-bye,

Lovingly,

Fanny.

Aubrey says Janet's portrait is by Rembrandt; but I tell him I don't think it was by a Frenchman at all, I think it was by Greuze.

Sorrow

A Letter

A Letter to Mrs. Carly, Florence, Italy.

New York, Wednesday.

My Dear Mary:

You were right when you said to me, two years ago, that the time would come when I would realize the futility, the selfish, the absurd insufficiency of my life. It is now six months since I lost my little girl—my only child. I thank you so much for your letter; I was sure you, who had so much heart, would realize more than most people what I suffered and feel still. And it needn't have been—I shall always maintain it *needn't* have been! She was overheated at dancing-school and caught cold coming home. I was late dressing for an early dinner, thought it was nothing, and paid no attention. From the dinner I went to the opera, from the opera to a ball, on to somebody else's. I was dead tired when I came home and fell into bed and asleep. All this time, my child, with her cold, was sleeping close beside an open window! The maid was careless, of course, but it wasn't *her* child—it was mine—and I hold myself most to blame. In two more days the doctor told me she couldn't live. I shall never forgive him! In six hours she was dead. I think I went quite mad. I know I really felt as if I had wantonly murdered her; and I still feel I was myself largely responsible. She was the dearest little creature! I am so sorry you never saw her. "I love my mamma best, and God next," she kept on saying all that last day. One wondered and wondered what thought was in her little brain. "You are mother's darling," I said to her—"mother's precious little girl, but God gave you to her, so you are God's first!" She threw her arms about my neck and kissed me, and said: "I like you better than all the little boys at dancing-school put together!" She fluttered about the bed with her arms like a little tired bird! She made me sing to her. I sang hours and hours—lullabies and comic songs she liked best. My maid came to me: "Madame is lunching out."

I was furious with her for coming to me with any such remark. "Telegraph!" was all I said. "Telegraph what, madame?"

"I don't care," I answered.

O my dear Mary! to watch a little soul going—a little soul that is all yours, or at least that you thought was all yours! To watch the light of life fade and fade out of a face precious to you, into which you cannot kiss the color again; to watch this little life, dearer to you than your own, slip, slip away from you in spite of your hands clutching to hold it back, or clasped in prayer to keep it! To sit and lose and be helpless! Oh, the agony of it! Marie came once more; it was dark; I guessed her errand, and only looked at her. She went away without a word. I took the child out of the bed—it was like lifting a flower. At dawn she died in my arms. Oh, were ever arms so empty as when they hold the dead body of someone loved?

And then began the revelations. The stilted letters of condolence, written with exactly the same amount of feeling as a note of regrets or acceptance, and couched very much in the same sort of language.

One woman recommended her dressmaker as being the most *chic* woman in New York for mourning—as if I cared! A great many cards were left at the door with their corners turned down, and for awhile no invitations came. That was all! Most of the people I was unfortunate enough to meet made such remarks as— —

"My Dear Mrs. Emery, I am so sorry to hear of your loss" (as if the house had been burned down or the silver plate had been stolen); or else— —

"Dear Mrs. Emery, I was so shocked to hear it; such a *sweet* child! Which was it, a boy or a girl? Oh, yes, I remember, a boy—a nice creature; but, my dear, so many boys turn out badly. You must try and console yourself with thinking perhaps you have both been saved a world of trouble after all!"

"My child was a little girl," I answered.

Another woman came to me, saying:

"You poor, dear thing! I'm glad you are bearing it so well—you look splendidly. Of course you won't stay in mourning long; will you? It's really not necessary for a child; and then I think one *needs* the distractions of society to drown one's sorrows!"

And all in such a flippant tone!

There are some who haven't heard of it at all, which seems so strange to me, who see and think of nothing else indoor and out!

And Sue Troyon I shall never forget or stop loving as long as I live. She put her arms about me and kissed me, when she first met me, right in the street, and never said a word, but her eyes were wet. *She* is a woman and a friend!

So now I am going to join you abroad, to travel and live among pictures and music and real people. These months out of society have broken the charm. I've tried to go back, but I can't stand it. The inanities of an afternoon At Home are more than I can bear. Everybody repeating to each other the same absurd commonplaces over and over again. Society conversation in one way is like a Wagner opera: it is composed of the same themes, which recur over and over again; only, in the conversation referred to, these themes are deadly, dull, fatuous remarks. As for balls and evening parties, I don't care about dancing any more, somehow, and to see the young *débutantes* about me almost breaks my heart, full of memories of my daughter and what she might have been. Tears are not becoming to a very low-necked dress, and shouldn't be worn with powder and jewels. No, my dear Mary, I see in this society of ours, we all grow so hardened, that if we don't have some such grief as I have had, we become hopeless. People soon forgot I had ever had a child, or at least that she hadn't been dead for years. I find myself becoming a bore, because of perhaps a certain lack of spirit that I used to have; and I began to realize that I had never been liked for myself, but for what I gave, and for the atmosphere of amusement which I helped to create by nearly always being gay and enjoying myself. As you yourself said of society, it is absolutely unsatisfactory. I never knew a purely society woman yet who wasn't somewhat or sometimes dissatisfied. First, they can't go as much or everywhere they want; and soon after they have all the opportunities they desire, they find that isn't sufficient, after all, to make life perfect, and then the boredom of fatigue begins to creep upon them with the years, and soon old age begins like a worm to eat into what happiness they have had.

Oh, no! When I think of how full your life is, of the interesting people you know—not merely empty names with a fashionable address or a coronet on their note paper, — of the places you see and the books you read; and then hear you say your life is too short to see or enjoy a third the world has to offer you! You happy, *happy* woman you!

Well! The house is for sale! What furniture I want to keep stored! John, who is prematurely old and half-dead with trying to earn enough money to keep us going as we wished in New York, has entered into it all in exactly my spirit. He has sold his seat on the stock exchange. He has disposed of all his business interests here. We find we have quite enough income to travel as long as we like, moderately, and to live abroad for as many years as we please. When we get homesick — as we are both sure to, for after all we are good Americans — we will come back here and settle down quietly in some little house, near everybody, but not in the whirlpool — on the banks of society, as it were, so that when we feel like it we can go and paddle in it for a little, just over our ankles. Two weeks after you receive this letter you will receive us! We sail on *Kaiser Wilhelm* to Naples.

No one here knows what to make of us! It's absurd the teapot tempest we've created. The verdict finally is that we've either lost our money or else our minds!

With a heart full of love,

Affectionately,

Agnes.

The Theatre

Four Letters, a Bill, and a Quotation from a Newspaper

I

A Letter from Mrs. Frederick Strong to her Husband.

... Fifth Avenue, Saturday.

My Dear Fred:

You must come home at once. Dick has announced his engagement to an actress—a soubrette, too, in a farce-comedy. If it had been a woman who played Shakespeare, it would have been bad enough, but a girl who sings and dances and does all sorts of things, including wearing her dresses up-side down, as it were—that is, too high at the *bottom* and too *low* at the top—well, this is a little too much!—just as we were getting a really good position in society. If the marriage isn't put a stop to, you can be sure she'll soon dance and kick us out of any position whatever that's worth holding. It isn't as if we had any one to back us; but you never had any family, and the least said about mine the better, so we have to be our own ancestors. And just as we had succeeded in getting a footing, in placing ourselves so that our children will be all right, your brother must go and do his best to ruin it all! You see how necessary it is for you to be on the spot. We may be able to break the engagement off before it is too late. Leave the mine to take care of itself, or go to pieces if need be. One mine more or less won't make any difference to us. Besides, you must think of your children! Your brother, too; he's sure to regret it.

I am ill over this thing. Can't sleep, and have frightful indigestion. Everybody's talking about it, and the newspapers are full this morning. My new costume came home from Mme. V— —'s yesterday; but there's no pleasure now in wearing it!

With love,

Annie.

January 19th.

And the ball we were going to give next month! What about the ball? Mrs. W— — had promised me we should have some of the smartest people here! This will ruin everything. Telegraph me when you will come. I am suicidal.

II

A Bill.

Mr. Fred'k Strong, Dr.

To the — — Private Detective Agen-
cy, for services rendered, $— — —.

                              Rec'd payment,   — — —

Feb. 10th, 189–.

III

*A Letter from Miss Beatrice North to Richard Strong, sent by special de-
livery to his Club.*

February 11th.

My Darling Dick:

What is the meaning of this letter from a lawyer? Who has been trying to damage my character? To ruin my happiness? Who hates me? I have never willingly harmed any one. I can't and won't believe this letter was sent with your approval. But why didn't you come to see me yesterday? My dearest in the world, you wouldn't believe evil stories of me, surely! You to whom I have told all my life, everything, for there has been nothing to hide. No, no; I am sure you don't know anything about this cruel letter, and for God's sake hurry and tell me so yourself, hurry and tell me so, and let me kiss the words as they come to your lips.

Thine,

Beatrice.

IV

Letter from the Same to the Same.

The evidence that you have proves nothing whatever, and even then much of it is exaggerated, which I, in my turn, can prove. I shall sue you for breach of promise.

Beatrice North.

V

From the Same to the Same, a day later.

I will not write to your lawyers. This second letter of theirs is too insulting. They know very well they could never win the case against me. (I am innocent; and even if I were not, your evidence is ridiculously insufficient.) And that is why they offer to "settle" with me privately. But my own feelings have changed over night. That you could, first, believe the charges against me, and second, that you could have allowed me to be insulted by your—*or your broth-er's*—lawyers, as you have done, these two things have opened my eyes to your own weak contemptible character. I am grateful the discovery came before it was too late. I release you from your engagement to me, and far from bringing a suit against you I feel I owe you a debt of thanks. I trust this is a sufficient reply to your insult to "settle" privately. The matter is at end with this letter.

Beatrice North.

VI

Headlines of a Column in a Daily New York Paper.

THE STRONG'S BALL!
ALL THE SWELLS THERE!
DICK STRONG GETS THE COLD
SHOULDER FROM MOST
OF HIS FRIENDS!

Mrs. Sternwall's Box. The First Act of Tristan and Isolde is three-quarters over. Mr. Alfred Easterfelt is seated alone in the corner. He is bored.

MR. ALFRED EASTERFELT.

(*To himself, after a long sigh.*) Damn it! What did I come so early for?

(*People are heard by the entire audience entering the little ante-room behind. The men's chorus on the stage drowns the sound of artificial laughter. The curtains part, and* Mr. Easterfelt *is joined by* Mrs. Sternwall, Mrs. Morley, Miss Beebar, *and* Mr. Carn.)

MRS. MORLEY.

(*Seriously.*) What a pity we've missed so much.

(*There are general greetings, whispered pleasantly. Each person, without exception, glances first all about the house, and then turns his eyes slowly toward stage. Mrs. Sternwall sits in the corner, facing the audience with three-quarters face, as the photographers express it, one-quarter toward the singers and* mise en scène. *She beckons Easterfelt to sit behind her. The others fall into the other places more or less as they happen, the women in front looking lovely, as each one is well aware, with her beautiful white neck, her jewels, and her charming coif. The music continues.*)

MRS. MORLEY.

(*Suddenly noticing that Mr. Sternwall is not with them.*) But where is Mr. Sternwall?

MRS. STERNWALL.

Oh, Henry always goes across to Hammerstein's Olympia during the acts, but he will join us for each of the entre-acts.

(*She takes up her opera glass, and examines the house minutely.*)

MISS BEEBAR.

What is the opera?

MRS. MORLEY.

Tristan and Isolde. I don't care for the new woman; do you? Somehow she hasn't the soul for Wagner. She sings well enough, mechanically, but she doesn't feel enough.

MISS BEEBAR.

Precisely. That's a wig of course; isn't it? And what an ugly one!

MRS. STERNWALL.

(*Low to Mr. Easterfelt.*) Come to-morrow at four. He has taken to leaving the office much earlier the last few days.

(*Owing to a sudden pause in the music, her voice has been heard quite distinctly. She is embarrassed for a moment, to cover which she leans over toward Mrs. Morley and Miss Beebar.*)

I wish Eames sang in this, she wears such good clothes.

MR. CARN.

What's that about Eames?

MISS BEEBAR.

I thought Eames' name would wake you up!

MR. CARN.

I was listening to the music.

MISS BEEBAR.

Don't be absurd; you know you never come to hear the opera, except when I am going.

MR. CARN.

Or when Eames sings.

MISS BEEBAR.

Ah! you acknowledge it! You brute!

MR. CARN.

It's her arms, and her eyes, and her hair. You must acknowledge she's very beautiful — —

MISS BEEBAR.

(*Interrupts.*) For heaven's sake stop; you bore me to death. Besides you must listen. It isn't the thing to talk at the opera any more.

(*Isolde gives Tristan the cup with the love potion in it.*)

MRS. STERNWALL.

(*In a very low voice to Mr. Easterfelt.*) Just before the curtain falls change your position quietly. Go near Miss Beebar and Mrs. Morley, on account of Henry. He will come to the box the minute the lights are turned up.

MISS BEEBAR.

(*Very low to Mr. Carn.*) I *hate* Eames!

MR. CARN.

No. (*He kisses, without sound, her bare shoulders.*)

(*Tristan and Isolde approach each other with outstretched arms. For the first time Mrs. Morley takes her gaze from the stage. It rests upon a dim figure in a certain seat in the Opera Club's box. Her eyes are full of tears.*)

A Perfect Day

A Leaf from the Diary of Mrs. Herbert Dearborn, Living in Paris

May −, 1897.

A charming, delightful day! Marie brought me my coffee at nine, as usual, with a perfect mail. No nasty business letters from America, but only most desirable invitations, notes full of gossip, and regrets from the Thompsons for the expensive dinner I felt obliged to give them at *Armenonville,* so I won't have to give it! One's old friends in America are really rather a bother, coming to Paris in the very middle of the season. If they came only in midsummer, when every one is away, one would be very glad to do what one could, if one were in the city. Of course, as far as the Thompsons themselves are concerned, I love them. My coffee never tasted so deliciously, and Marie said I looked unusually well after my night's rest. To be sure Marie says that every morning; but never mind, it is always pleasant to hear the first thing one wakes up, and I only wish I didn't have a sneaking fear that the new Empire pink bed-hangings help a good deal. Marie sprayed the room with my new perfume (a secret; no one else has it), laved my face in rose-water, and then I had a wee little nap by way of a starter for the day. After my bath I answered my mail; and then, Marie having manicured my nails, my toilet was made. I wore, to go out, my striking blue costume, with the hat and sun-shade to match, which always necessitates the greatest care with the complexion. I use an entirely different powder with this dress, and one has to be most careful about one's cheeks. But Marie is invaluable so far as the complexion is concerned, and I went out quite satisfied. First, to the hair-dresser's to have my hair re-dyed, as I went to the races in the afternoon, and the light there is very trying. Unless your hair has been dyed very lately it is quite useless to go. My hair was never done so well. I am trying it a very little darker, and I am almost sure I like it better. Then I went into some shops. I think it is always a good thing to have one's carriage seen waiting outside the smart shops often. I priced a great many things, and had several—which I of course have no idea whatever of buying—sent home on approval. To the dressmaker's, to try on my new dress. It was finished; but didn't suit me. I am having entirely new sleeves and all the trimming changed.

I persuaded them it was their fault. I had really thought I should like it that way until I saw it completed. Then to breakfast with the Countess of − −; a charming *déjeuner*. All the women very desirable to know and very *chicly* dressed, and not one looking so young for their age, I am sure, as I. In fact, several made that remark to me. I know they say just the opposite behind my back, but it is pleasant to hear nice things under any circumstances. I think it is all one should ask of people, that they should be nice to our faces. I left *déjeuner* first, because that makes a good impression, as if you are crowded with engagements, and flatters your hostess, who is naturally pleased to catch a much-sought-after guest. I really drove home to rest a little before the races. I find taking off *everything* and indulging in complete relaxation, if only for ten minutes, is wonderfully refreshing, and saves lots of *lines*! While I was resting my *masseur* came and gave me face massage. There is nothing like it for a wrinkle-destroyer. And the man is a rather nice person who amuses me. I got him two new clients at the luncheon today. As the other women said, one is only too willing to pay extra to get a man who is good-looking.

The races were very exciting. It was a lovely day, our coach had a fine position, and our party was much stared at! I had the most conspicuous seat, and did my best to become it. It isn't for me to say to myself if I succeeded or not, but I owe it to my dress-maker to make the statement that no one else had on a better gown. I wish that statement was the only thing I owed him! I won forty louis; I don't know how. I am absolutely ignorant about horses. I only go because it seems to be the thing to do now. But I thought one of the jockeys looked rather fetching, and so I put my money on him, and he happened to win.

We all went for tea to Mrs. − −'s, where one of the most expensive singers sang. But I didn't hear her, because if you go into the music room you have to sit down in rows, and you don't see any of the people.

I was obliged to hurry away, as my appointment with Jacques today was for 6:30, and I wanted to stop at an imitation jeweller's place in the rue de la Paix, where I had heard were some wonderful paste necklaces. They are quite extraordinary. I ordered one, and shall never tell a soul it's not real. I was late home, but Jacques, the dear boy, was waiting, and seemed to me sweeter than ever this afternoon. I gave him the cuff links I have had made for him, with his initials in rubies, and it was too delightful to see his pleasure. I took him out to dine. I think I will marry him. I know he is much younger than I, and all that, but he's so sweet, and, after all, I have enough money for two.

The Westington's "Bohemian Dinner"

A Letter

The Sherwood

58 West 57th St.

My Dear Dora:

We are just home from dining in one of the smartest houses in New York, and I've been bored so wide awake I can't think of going to bed, so I am sitting in my petticoat (that charming white silk, much-festooned, and many-flounced one you brought me over from Paris) and a dressing sack (pink, not so very unbecoming). My hair is down, but Dick doesn't paint it any more — it's getting thin, dear! — and I've nice little swansdown lined slippers over my best white silk-stockings. I've worn to-night the best of everything my wardrobe affords, and I wasn't ashamed of myself! No, I was much more ashamed of the Westingtons, and I'm going to tell you all about it before I touch the pillow! I'm sure you'll be amused.

In the first place, to be honest, we were rather pleased to be asked. There is no one smarter than the W.'s, and, besides, they are attractive and good-looking. The truth is, we've always been anxious to go to their house — heaven knows why, now that we've been. We are sufficiently punished, however, for being so foolish as to be flattered by our invitation. For, my dear, we weren't asked to a swell dinner at all; we were invited to what was intended for a "Bohemian" affair (but it was only a dull and ungainly one), and it was apparently taken for granted that, as Dick painted and I hadn't millions, we were decidedly eligible. Of course, as you know, there is no such thing as a real Bohemia in New York.

The dinner was given in honor (apparently) of the Hungarian pianist Romedek and his wife. He has been an enormous success here this year, and society has taken him up. But the trouble is with Madame Romedek; no one is sure she *is* Madame Romedek, and a great many people are sure she isn't. She is a pretty, rather common-looking person, with no particular intelligence or *esprit*. I am told she is more communicative *under* the table than she is over it; and I know some men are crazy about her. Of course, she isn't a woman any of us can stand for a moment. If Romedek were a painter we should know she'd been his model, and be awfully sorry for him. But Romedek is a musician (a great one—I wish you could hear him); and they say she hasn't even the social prestige or poetic license of having been an artist's model, but of having been something quite wrong to begin with. Naturally, you see, some of society won't have her at any price. Those that must have *him* have difficulty in entertaining them. I hear one prominent woman who was asked last week to dine and meet the Romedeks considered herself insulted, and has struck her would-be hostess' name off her visiting list. So you see it wasn't all plain sailing with the Westington's, and I can hear them decide between themselves to give a "real Bohemian dinner;" that is, ask people who "do things," and whom you sometimes do meet out at houses where they are not particular about mixing—the kind of people who would probably not take offense at being asked to meet Mrs. Romedek without having her marriage certificate for their dinner card. Of course, as you know, I don't mind being asked to meet anybody. Thank goodness! I feel perfectly secure about my reputation, and also about my position, which is quite good enough to please me. But there is a difference in being asked to meet a questionable person because that person is brilliant, or beautiful, or talented, and that therefore you (belonging to the aristocracy of brains) will appreciate her, and, on the other hand, being asked to meet her because you are an artist's wife and don't mind that sort of thing. We *do* mind it very much! We don't even *care* for it in geniuses—only we overlook it in a genius; disregard it as not being our affair. But to be asked to meet a silly, loose woman with the idea that I won't mind, almost as if I approved, I resent that.

However, let me tell you who was there. On Mrs. Westington's right, of course, sat Romedek, and he is very handsome and very charming, and I think at least Mrs. Westington enjoyed her dinner if nobody else did. On Mrs. W.'s left was Mr. — —, who is, you know, a great swell here and who poses as being a fast patron of the arts and graces—especially the graces—after the pattern of a Frenchman who has his *entrée* behind the scenes of the opera. His wife never accepts invitations that he does; they meet, you know, under their own roof, for the sake of the children—but under their *own* roof only. So in her place Belle Carterson was asked, who has gone in for keeping a swell florist's place, and they say is making money. She is independent, and I like her, but of course it is considered by her friends in society that since she went in for business she can't refuse to meet *anyone*. Dick sat next to her, and had on the other side of him Mrs. — —, who likes celebrities without the knack of selection, and whose invitations nowadays I believe are never accepted at once, but are kept open as long as possible to see if something better won't turn up. Then came Mrs. Romedek and Mr. Westington; he looking bored to death, and she as if she didn't know where she was at. Then Bobbie Lawsher, who writes books and operettas and things—rather amusing he is, but becoming more and more of a snob every day. It's bad enough to see a woman straining every nerve to get into society, but when you see a man it's worse than ridiculous. I met him at a smart party the other night, and he stuck by me for hours, asking who everybody was till I lost my patience and told him I couldn't be a Blue Book for him or anybody, and he would either have to dance with me at once or go to some one else with his questions. I never knew any one who could bring in the names of as many smart people in one short remark as Bobbie can. If you happen to ask him what time it is, you could make a wager that, in his answer, in a perfectly natural way, he will mention familiarly three smart society women (calling one at least by her first name). Of course he does get asked a great deal, because he's little more than a snub-cushion—holds any amount of them as easily as pins. Besides he goes to afternoon bores, like Teas and At Homes and Days, for which free and untrammelled men can only be obtained by subterfuge and trick or some extraordinary bribe. To a young man like Bobbie Lawsher afternoon affairs are a sort of happy hunting ground, a social grab bag, where he can never be sure there isn't a dinner invitation, or one for the opera, or a luncheon, to be secured if one is clever and careful. Why, when a woman has a man guest back out at the last moment from a dinner, the first thing she does is to rush off to any At Home, that's going on, with the fairly confident expectation of finding Bobbie Lawsher and making him fill her vacancy. Bobbie has accomplishments of a certain sort, can sing a pretty little song in a pretty little way, and can pass a tea cup without spilling, and drink tea himself, and can hang around when he's wanted, and be got rid of easily when he isn't. He is a sort of society errand boy, and very useful. I take it back about his having accomplishments—a better word for them is *conveniences*!

Well, on the other side of Bobbie was Mrs. — —, red in the face, so angry she was asked to meet Madame Romedek, talking with poor Bobbie in a sharp, spasmodic sort of way, as if she were carrying on the conversation with her knife and fork, cutting the sentences into bits, some ignoring and some eating,—and none agreeing with her, or she agreeing with none. Then George Ringold asked, I suppose, for me. I am quite aware that women who are indiscreet themselves think there is "more than meets the eye" between George and me. I am very fond of him, and so is Dick. And he has kissed me, and Dick knows it; but I am sure I need not tell you that is all. On the other side was Romedek, and perhaps I ought to feel complimented, but as, thanks to Mrs. Westington, we didn't succeed in carrying on to a finish any single conversation we started, I don't allow myself to be too flattered.

Mrs. W. talked music, of course—the commonplaces of it—such as any well-bred, smart, educated woman of the world knows how to talk nowadays, with perhaps just one good, big, absurd mistake thrown in,—thus, by the grace of humor keeping banality from becoming absolutely fatal. Madame Romedek was rather amusing. She tried to be the lady—which, as she doesn't know how, and only succeeds in being impossibly stupid, must have bored the men on each side of her tremendously. That's where foolish women of that sort spoil their own game. If they would make the best of the bargain, and be frankly a common cocotte *gone right*, they would certainly be more amusing, and might have something like success, at any rate with the men.

The food was excellent, the wine good, the house lovely! And as soon after dinner as was at all decent, we left. We decided in the cab on our way home, from no point of view had it paid,—financially least of all; for our dinner in the restaurant, with all our jolly friends, would have cost us only seventy-five cents, while our cab bill for the evening was three dollars. As for having had a good time, there was only one person there who had that—Mrs. Westington herself. I believe even the servants must have been bored by the dinner, unless, perhaps, Madame Romedek flirted with *them*; which I should think extremely likely.

I am getting sleepy now, of which fact my letter undoubtedly bears "internal evidence." So good night and sweet dreams to you, and none to me—I don't like them!

Write me what you are doing in Paris. I am sure your husband will have his usual great success in the Champ de Mars. We are all very proud of him.

With love, dear Dora,

Guenne Barrows.

- Madame Eugenie Leblanche, veuve, age 62 years.
- Mlle. Nina and Mlle. Fifi.
- Mrs. Henry B. Gording and Mrs. Wm. H. Lane.
- Mme. Borté and Mme. Lautre.

I

The Baccarat Table in the Villa des Fleurs, Aix-les-Bains.

MADAME EUGENIE LEBLANCHE, *veuve.*

(A large, stout lady in black satin and brocade, violet-colored face-powder, and a reddish blonde display underneath a questionable bonnet. She wears a somewhat profuse and miscellaneous display of jewels, principally diamonds dull as the eyes of dissipation. She holds her chips in large loose white cotton gloves that reach to her elbow. Her lips, compressed together, move constantly, with a sort of excited switch-back motion.)

(To herself.) I wonder who has the cards. Oh, it's that monsieur there, I see. Not good! I will only place two louis. (*She asks the gentleman in front of her to place them for her. He does so.*) No, I am wrong, I will put three. (*She asks the gentleman to place a third louis for her. In doing so the chip rolls from his fingers; he immediately recaptures it and places it properly.*) Monsieur, monsieur, if you please. Return me my louis, if you please! I never play a louis that has rolled on the table. That would bring us bad fortune, you would see! Thank you, thank you very much. (*To herself again.*) I am sorry I did not ask him to hand me back two. We are going to lose! Good heavens! it is sure we lose! Ah, the cards! Bad, that's sure! O, what emotion! O good heavens! Seven! But the bank! No, we gain! O— — O good heavens! Good heavens! what emotion! We gain! What a misfortune I didn't leave the extra louis! It is disgusting! I regret it now. O, I regret it very much! But it is always like that with me! Are we going to be paid? I don't think so! No, we won't be paid! It is always like that; when one loses one is taken, and when one wins one is never paid! O good heavens! Now he will pay our side. After all there ought to be enough money. O yes, yes, we will be paid! All the better! Two

louis for me if you please, thank you. Monsieur, I am sorry to trouble you to give me my four louis! No, no, you haven't given me enough! I put down two louis. O yes, you are right. Pardon me, I didn't understand; yes, I have four. Thank you very much. You are very kind. (*To herself again.*) I am paid! After all, I am paid! So much the better! What emotion! I will play two louis again; no, three; no, two; no, one must have courage. Monsieur, if you please, will you have the kindness to place my four louis on the table? Thank you very much! (*To herself again.*) But, if I lose! and I will lose. Good heavens! O— — what emotion! (*Etc., etc.*)

II

MLLE. NINA.

(*Young, very beautiful, in an exquisite gown from Laferiere, with gorgeous jewels and a wonderful hat.*)

Who is the banker?

MLLE. FIFI.

(*Equally charming, as magnificently jeweled, and as exquisitely gowned; also a chapeau of wonderful birds, such as never sang in any wood.*)

He? He is an old Russian. He has millions and millions, my dear!

MLLE. NINA.

(*Raising her eyebrows and regarding the banker affectionately.*) Really?

MLLE. FIFI.

Yes, yes; and he is a perfect gentleman. He gave Lala of the Vaudeville three strings of pearls in two days. He is very generous and altogether nice.

MLLE. NINA.

(*Jealously.*) Do you know him?

MLLE. FIFI.

O no, my dear; he is not my style. You know I never like a gentleman who parts his hair on the left side. It's my fad.

MLLE. NINA.

(*Very pleasantly.*) Have you won to-night, dearie?

MLLE. FIFI.

Ah, yes, my dear! *Think!* two thousand francs already!

MLLE. NINA.

(*Very sweetly, moving away.*) So much the better. I've lost like the devil. (*She very slowly makes a detour of the table in the direction of the Russian banker. At the same time an elderly gentleman approaches Mlle. Fifi and speaks to her.*)

LE MONSIEUR.

Good evening, my dear!

MLLE. FIFI.

Good evening, my pig of a Prince!

LE MONSIEUR.

You have won?

MLLE. FIFI.

Oh, but *no*, my dear! I have lost *enormously*! It is *terrible* what I've done! I have lost nearly *all* I have!

MLLE. NINA.

(*Who has just arrived behind the banker, leaning over his shoulder and watching him win an enormous coup.*) Ah, ha! You see, Monsieur, I bring you good fortune always!

THE BANKER.

I didn't know you were behind me, mademoiselle. (*He looks up. She smiles sweetly and innocently. He is pleased.*)

MLLE. NINA.

Oh, yes, for a long time!

THE BANKER.

You don't play?

MLLE. NINA.

(*With a manner altogether modest, and a soft, low voice.*) Oh, no; never! I have nothing to risk; besides, it doesn't amuse me very much. I never play.

THE BANKER.

Put on that hundred francs just to try your fortune.

MLLE. NINA.

(*Leaning over, takes the note from the pile.*) If you wish it. (*She plays and wins; brushes his cheek and shoulder with her arm as she reaches over to take up her money.*)

(*The play continues.*)

MLLE. NINA.

(*Still winning.*) You know you are very nice. (*She plays again with a note from the banker's pile.*)

III

MRS. HENRY B. GORDING, *of Rochester, New York.*

Do you play?

MRS. WM. H. LANE, *of Brooklyn.*

No, not really. I don't quite approve of it, but I just try my luck once in awhile for amusement.

MRS. HENRY B. GORDING.

Yes, that's exactly the way I feel. So long as you don't go in for it seriously I don't see any harm.

MRS. WM. H. LANE.

And if you stop as soon as you begin to lose.

MRS. HENRY B. GORDING.

Yes, indeed! Oh my! are you putting one down?

MRS. WM. H. LANE.

Yes, I think that man looks lucky over there with the glasses; besides I like him because his wife sits right by him all the evening.

MRS. HENRY B. GORDING.

(*Smiling nervously and fumbling in her glove where she has concealed the money to have it conveniently ready.*) Put one down for me, too; will you? (*She smiles hysterically.*) Dear me, I wonder what my husband would say if he could see me?

MRS. WM. H. LANE.

I don't know a single thing about the game; do you?

MRS. HENRY B. GORDING.

(*With two small red spots coming into her cheeks.*) Not the slightest. It's finished! I wonder who's won!

MRS. WM. LANE.

(*After a long excited sigh.*) I don't know. I never can tell till I see them either taking up our chips, or else paying us!

MRS. HENRY B. GORDING.

(*Breathlessly.*) If I lose, I shall go.

MRS. WM. H. LANE.

So shall I! We've won!

MRS. HENRY B. GORDING.

Ah! — — — —.

MRS. WM. H. LANE.

(*Looking at least ten years older than she did two minutes before.*) No, we've lost!

MRS. HENRY B. GORDING.

O! — — — —.

MRS. WM. H. LANE.

I'm not going. I shall try once more!

MRS. HENRY B. GORDING.

So shall I.

MRS. WM. H. LANE.

And I don't believe the woman is that man's wife after all. If she had been we wouldn't have lost our dollars!

IV

MME. BORTÉ.

(*Leaning over a man's right shoulder for some gold on the table.*) I beg pardon; that is my two louis!

MME. LAUTRE.

(*Leaning over the man's left shoulder.*) But no, madame, it is mine! I put a louis down there!

MME. BORTÉ.

No, no! That is where I put mine. Give me my louis!

MME. LAUTRE.

But you are wrong, madame; it is my louis, and I shall keep it!

MME. BORTÉ.

But no, madame!

MME. LAUTRE.

But yes— —!

THREE WOMEN BESIDE MME. BORTÉ.

Yes, madame is right. She certainly put a louis down there.

THE SAME NUMBER OF WOMEN BESIDE MME. LAUTRE.

No, it is the other madame who put the money down there.

A MAN ON THE OPPOSITE SIDE OF THE TABLE.

Ssss— —

UN MONSIEUR.

Oh, the women! the women!—always rowing!

CROUPIER.

Make your plays, gentlemen!

MME. LAUTRE AND MME. BORTÉ.

(*Together; each to her own coterie.*) You know perfectly it is my louis; isn't it? Oh, never in my life! Never! never!

(*The game continues, and so does the discussion.*)

PRINTED AT THE LAKESIDE PRESS,
CHICAGO, FOR THE PUBLISHERS,
HERBERT S. STONE & CO. CHICAGO, U.S.A.